Simonetta Perkins

Simonetta Perkins

L.P. Hartley

ET REMOTISSIMA PROPE

Hesperus Classics

Hesperus Classics
Published by Hesperus Press Limited
4 Rickett Street, London sw6 1ru
www.hesperuspress.com

Simonetta Perkins first published in 1925
First published by Hesperus Press Limited, 2004

Copyright © The Estate of L.P. Hartley, 1925
Foreword © Margaret Drabble, 2004

The Estate of L.P. Hartley asserts the moral right of L.P. Hartley to be identified
as the Author of *Simonetta Perkins*.

isbn: 1-84391-091-8

CONTENTS

FOREWORD

L.P. Hartley fell in love with Venice in 1922 when he was a young man, and this novella, *Simonetta Perkins*, is a tribute to his lasting passion. Venice has inspired innumerable love affairs, in life and in art, many of them tragic: Henry James's *The Wings of a Dove* (1902) and Thomas Mann's *Death in Venice* (1912) represent a still-thriving literary genre of doomed and frustrated romance. Hartley's story, in contrast, has optimism and spirit. It deals with a rash, unsuitable and unrequited love, but it has a youthful lightness of touch that offers the possibility of a better future for its heroine. Lavinia Johnstone does not give in to her respectable fate without protest.

Leslie Poles Hartley (1895–1972) was homosexual, and, like his near-contemporary E.M. Forster, in his fiction he tended to transform homosexual into heterosexual romance, in deference to the conventions of the period. Just as the wealthy young Bostonian Lavinia chooses the name 'Simonetta Perkins' as an alibi and a disguise, so Hartley disguises his own love for a handsome gondolier by using the persona of the marriageable but obstinate Lavinia. Lavinia has been brought to Venice by her formidable mother on a Grand Tour, having rejected various eligible suitors at home, and she has seriously applied herself to informed sightseeing and to an inner debate with Ruskin about the architectural merits of churches and paintings. Hartley himself visited Venice, not with his mother, but with a succession of gay friends, including the novelist C.H.B. Kitchin and the biographer and critic David Cecil. From 1927, he rented an apartment in Venice from a baroness (he loved titles) and took into his employment the gondolier Pietro Busetti, with whom he maintained an affectionate relationship for years. His affair with Venice was more than a holiday romance.

Simonetta Perkins was Hartley's first short apprentice novel, in which he tried out several of the themes that were to emerge more fully in the work of his maturity. When it appeared in 1925, he had already published one volume of short stories, *Night Fears* (1924), and had made a name for himself as a reviewer. He was on friendly terms with many literary and social figures, including Lady Ottoline Morrell, Margot Asquith, and the Sitwells. He was a man of the midlands, of delicate health, independent means and middle-class Wesleyan Methodist descent, and, like many of his characters, he was a social climber with a *nostalgie de la boue*. Virginia Woolf described him as 'a dull fat man', but others found him excellent and entertaining company. The mixture of diffidence and confidence displayed by his heroine Lavinia seems to have been very much part of his own personality: shy, prone to feelings of guilt and self-doubt, he nevertheless had enough determination to carry him onwards into a successful career and at least some accommodation of his own sexual preferences. Unlike that other Venice-obsessed gay fantasist, Frederick William Rolfe (1860–1913), he never plunged recklessly into the danger and squalor of the Venetian underworld – an underworld that Lavinia is allowed to glimpse near the Rialto through a fleeting moment of street violence. But he enjoyed the idea of it, and lived close enough to it to allow it to flourish attractively in his imagination.

Hartley's career as a novelist was not all plain sailing, despite his evident gifts and his instinctive cultivation of useful acquaintances. After the publication of *Simonetta Perkins* and another volume of short stories, *The Killing Bottle* (1932), he was discouraged for some years from writing fiction, feeling, according to David Cecil's account in the *Dictionary of National Biography*, that his works, 'though politely received, made no great impression'. But he did not give up, and went stubbornly on to build a solid reputation, producing many more novels, including his acknowledged masterpieces: the trilogy consisting of *The Shrimp and the Anemone* (1944), *The Sixth Heaven* (1946) and *Eustace and Hilda* (1947), and *The Go-Between* (1953), all of which deal with social aspiration, the British obsession with the class system, and the alluring dangers of sexual attraction across the social divide.

In the trilogy, we find some intriguing clues about the genesis of *Simonetta Perkins*. The hero Eustace Cherrington, a sensitive and delicate young man who desires to be a writer, is whisked off to Venice at the invitation of an aristocratic neighbour, Lady Nelly, in order to give him time to concentrate on his alleged work. She promises him 'No noise of traffic – just the soothing plash of the gondoliers' oars… Some Marco or Tito would be posted at your door with his finger on his lips. When inspiration flagged you could come out and stroll on the Piazza or bathe on the Lido.' Eustace struggles hard to resist the charms of Venice and to force himself to sit alone and write, but he succeeds, and against the odds produces what he describes as 'a short story, perhaps, a long short story, the kind no publisher would take'. But a publisher does take it, despite warning him that his 'Little Athens', being 40,000 words long, is a particularly difficult length to handle, 'so you must not expect any considerable sale'. Eustace announces his triumph to the old family housekeeper back home, saying proudly that a publisher has taken his novel: 'never mind,' she reassures him, 'you'll be able to get it back from him.'

We know that Hartley himself earned twelve pounds for

Simonetta Perkins, not a princely sum, but a sign of progress nevertheless. And the novella is well worth reading for its own sake. Hartley was always deeply moved by architecture, and here we find his impassioned youthful response to the 'cold rococo splendour of the Gesuiti, roofed and walled in gold'. The island of St Giorgio is 'the work of a magician', and Hartley and his heroine thrill to the purple waters of the canal, to the great span of the Rialto, and to the darkness in the thick foliage that shrouds the Casa Petrarca. The very language stirs them: Emilio the gondolier pronounces the words 'Palazzo Rezzonico' 'as though the name were heaven-sent, the explosive double z's so tamed and softened they might have fallen from the lips of an angel'. The physical grace and beauty of Emilio, with his sky-blue scarf and cascading sash, are described with an uninhibited admiration, and his poverty is evoked with a curious tenderness. The glory of Venice overwhelms the timidity and respectability of its English and American visitors, and offers the reader, as it offers Lavinia, 'a vision of high hopes, adventure, beauty, pomp, in the morning of the world' – a vision she may not fulfil, but knows she will never regret.

– Margaret Drabble, 2004

Simonetta Perkins

1

'Love is the greatest of the passions,' Miss Johnstone read, 'the first and the last.'

She lifted her eyes from the book, and they rested on the grey dome of Santa Maria della Salute, rising like a blister out of the inflamed and suppurating stonework below. The waters of the canal were turbid, bringing the church uncomfortably close. 'How I hate Baroque,' thought Miss Johnstone. 'And this, I am told, is the best example of it. It comes of being born in Boston, I suppose. And yet a Johnstone of Boston should be able to appreciate anything. Anything good, that is.'

She read on.

'Other passions tend to exaggerate and to intensify, but love transforms. The victim of the amorous passion has a holiday from himself. No longer does he discern in the objects he sees before him the pale reflection of his own mediocrity; those objects become the symbols of an inner quickening. An effulgence of the Absolute irradiates his being.'

'How often have I read this sort of thing before,' thought Miss Johnstone, trying to ignore the Salute, and fixing her gaze on the chaster outlines of St Gregory, across the way. 'Consider the servants here,' she soliloquised, glancing right and left along the sunny terrace whose steps were lapped by the waves; 'has any one of them, for any one moment, been irradiated by an effulgence of the Absolute? I think not.' She met the smirk of a passing concierge with a reproving stare. 'But they are all married, I suppose, or whatever in Venice takes the place of marriage.'

The print rose up at her, and she started once more to read.

'Love is an inheritance that falls to the lot of all mankind. Anger, envy, jealousy, cruelty; pity, charity, humility, courage:

3

these emotions are partial and unequal in their incidence. They visit some, and others they pass by. But man that is born of woman cannot escape love. Of whatsoever age thou art, reader, never believe thyself secure from his fiery dart.'

'Now here,' exclaimed Miss Johnstone, slamming the book face-downwards on the wicker-work table at her side, 'here, among much vapid rhetoric and dreary rubbish is one huge, dangerous, vital, misleading falsehood.'

This outburst having caused more than one lorgnette to be directed upon her, Miss Johnstone ceased to testify openly and continued her reflections to herself. But never had her whole consciousness, her whole being, shown itself, to her, so vociferously articulate. From her toes to her hair she was an incarnation of denial. 'It is a lie,' she thought, 'a cruel, useless lie. If I – since the writer, after many meaningless generalisations, now impudently addresses himself to me – if I had been capable of this passion, would not Stephen Seleucis and Michael B. Sprott and Theodore Drakenburg and Walt Watt have awakened it? They awakened it in everyone else, even in Mamma.' She looked round: but her mother had not yet appeared.

'The pinnacle of eligibility on which I sat, and to which in a month I must return, was, and no doubt again will be, festooned with offers of marriage. They affected me no more than an invitation to dinner, except that I was harassed by having to take some of them seriously. I am absolutely immune from love. If I marry, it will be from considerations of convenience.

'Alas that one cannot reply to an author except by making notes in the margin, notes he will never see! And this love-adept has wisely left his margins slender. Let me see what he says now. Aha! a threat!'

'In the case of solipsistical and egocentric natures, the tide of love, long awaited in secret' (Miss Johnstone frowned) 'may find a tortuous and uneasy passage. There is much to be absorbed, much to be overcome. The habit of self-communion must be subdued; all those private delights, the sense, so delicious to some, of retiring into oneself and drawing down the blinds, must be repudiated and foresworn. The unfortunate egoist must learn to take his pleasure from without; he is no longer his own warehouse and market-place, he must go out to buy. No longer may he think, "I will sit in such and such a position, it gives me ease"; or, "I will take a drive today and refresh my spirits", or, "tomorrow I will choose a suit of clothes"; for he will no longer find pleasure in the satisfaction of daily needs. Rather he will say, "If I rest my cheek thus upon my finger, how will Chloe regard it?" and, "I will wait upon Melissa with my barouche, though I abhor the motion", and, "since Julia is away I must go ragged and barefoot, for without her sanction I dare not choose either silk or shoe-leather". To such as have been accustomed to give others the first place in their thoughts, the oncoming of love will prove a bloodless revolution; but to the egoists, the epicures of their own sensations, the change will be violent, damaging and bitter.'

'Should I call myself an egoist?' Miss Johnstone mused. 'Others have called me so. They merely meant that I did not care for them. Now if they had said fastidious or discriminating! On the whole it is a pity that Stephen Seleucis is coming next week; but he did once say, "Lavinia, it isn't only your charm that attracts me, it's your refusal to see charm in anyone else. Even in me", he added. How could I contradict him? Certainly I am not selfish. Punctual myself, I am tolerant of unpunctuality in others. It is the mark of a saint, Walt Watt once told me. Why do I recall these foolish compliments?

They ought never to have found their way into my diary; and it is no answer to the author of this odious manual (who has somehow contrived to pique me) to urge that idle young men have talked as though they were in love with me. Can it be that I am vain? Why else should I have treasured those insinuating commendations? When Mamma speaks her mind to me, it goes like water off a duck's back.'

At that moment two visitors, both men, walked past her. One tilted his head back, as though his collar chafed him; but Miss Johnstone knew instinctively that he was indicating her, as, with an interrogatory lift of his voice he said,

'Beautiful?'

'Well, no,' his friend replied, 'not really beautiful.' They passed out of ear-shot. Miss Johnstone blinked, and involuntarily caught up the treatise upon Love, in her agitation forgetting to sneer at the opening words.

'Like all great subjects, love has its false prophets. You will hear men say, "I do not know whether I am in love or not"; but *your* heart, reader, will never give you this ambiguous answer. Doubtful symptoms there may be, excitement, irritability, sleeplessness, without cause shown; but uncertainty, when the eye of desire at last has the beloved object in its view, never.'

Miss Johnstone had recovered from her embarrassment. 'What execrable taste!' she exclaimed. 'The eye of desire, pooh!' She raised her own eyes, as though to record a protest to the heavens, but her outraged glance never climbed to the zenith. An intermediate object arrested it. Posted in front of her, though how it got there unobserved she could not imagine, a gondola lay rocking. At either end it was lashed to those blue posts whose function, apart from picturesqueness, Miss Johnstone for the first time dimly understood; and the gondolier was sitting on the poop and staring at the hotel. No, not at the hotel, decided Miss Johnstone, at me.

She tried to return the stare; it troubled her. It was vivid, abstracted, and unrecognising. It seemed to be projected up at her out of those fierce blue eyes.

She turned to look behind her, half expecting to see some dumb show, a servant making a face, that would explain the gondolier's interest and explain it away. She saw only a blind window and a blank wall. Unwillingly her eyes travelled back, searching vainly in their circuit for some less hazardous haven. Once more they rested on the gondolier. Hunched up, he sat, but without any appearance of awkwardness or of constriction; one brown hand drooped over his knee: the gold of his rings glittered against the brown. He was like some black bird that, in settling, had not troubled quite to fold its wings.

'But he can't really fly,' thought Miss Johnstone, meeting his eyes at last, 'and there's the water between us.' Emboldened by the reflection, she scanned his face. Did the twist of his brown moustache make him too predaceous, too piratical? She decided it did not. How did he come by the tawny hair that waved under the gallant curve of the black sombrero? Of course, many Venetians had brown hair. Again she dropped her eyes before the urgency of that stare, and at the same moment was conscious of a change in the demeanour of the loitering servants, and heard a familiar voice.

'Lavinia! Lavinia!' Right and left her mother's summons enfiladed the terrace. 'Am I to wait here all night?'

'Coming!' cried Miss Johnstone in a thin pipe, making her way through the occasional tables to where, nodding and tossing her bold, blonde head, her mother stood while the servants scurried round her.

'Where is my gondola?' that lady demanded, her eye sweeping the Grand Canal with such authority that her daughter thought the craft must rise, like Venus, from the waves. 'I ordered it for eleven. I come down at half-past eleven, and there is no sign of it.'

'Emilio, Emilio,' called a concierge, shrinking so much that his scarlet waistcoat hung quite loosely on him. 'He is here, Madam.'

'Why doesn't he come then, if he's here?' Mrs Johnstone asked, adding in a gentler tone, 'I see, he's untying himself. What unhandy things these gondolas are. No wonder they are to be abolished.'

Propelled from post to post by Emilio's outstretched hand the deprecated vessel drew up to the steps. With a gesture that just escaped being a flourish, the gondolier took off his hat and held it across his body; his hair blew backwards, caught by the wind. As though in a dream Miss Johnstone saw her mother, poised on the unsteady embarkation board, give him the benefit of that glare before which all Boston quailed; and then, a weakness surely without precedent, she saw her mother's eyelids flicker.

'*Comandi,*[1] *Signora?*' said the gondolier, whilst Miss Johnstone fitted herself into the space her mother left over.

'What does the man say?' asked Mrs Johnstone, petulant at being addressed in a foreign tongue.

'He wants to know where to take us,' Lavinia replied.

'Do you mean he doesn't know?' asked her mother, amazed that any wish of hers, however private, should be stillborn.

As though anxious to help, the gondolier came forward a little and leaned over them.

'*La chiesa dei Santi Giovanni e Paolo?*' he suggested. Soft and caressing, his voice lingered over the words as if he loved them.

'They always say that: they always take one there,'

pronounced Mrs Johnstone, implying that every Venetian conversation and destination was included in the gondolier's words. 'No, we will not go there. You have the book, Lavinia; what does it says for the third day?'

'I'm afraid we haven't kept pace with it,' Lavinia said. 'We should have to start out at daybreak. And the churches all shut at twelve. Let's go down the Grand Canal to the Rialto, and back by the little canals.'

'Tell him, then,' said Mrs Johnstone, settling herself against the cushions.

'*Gondoliere,*' Lavinia began, in a hesitating tone, as if she were about to ask his opinion on some private matter. She turned round to find his face close to hers; the beringed left hand, lying across his knee, was level with her eyes. 'How everyone in Venice seems to strike an attitude,' she thought, and the sentence she had prepared dissolved in her mind. She eked out her order with single words and vague gesticulations. Off sped the gondola; the palaces slid by; now they were under the iron bridge; soon they would be at the great bend. 'This man is a champion, my dear,' remarked Mrs Johnstone, 'he knows how to put the pace on.' Never before had Lavinia's mother so cordially approved of anything Venetian. But Lavinia herself wondered whether such purposefulness was quite in keeping with the spirit of the place. 'He has not mastered the art of languor,' she murmured. 'Art of what, Lavinia?' Mrs Johnstone challenged, stirring under her silks. 'Oh, nothing, Mamma.' For the thousandth time Lavinia climbed down. Just then they overtook a barge, piled high with lemons and tomatoes; the bargeman, impaled as it seemed on his punt-pole and shining with sweat, yet found it in him to turn and hail, in the sociable Italian fashion, the Johnstones' gondolier. The gorgeous fruits framed his glittering smile, and their abundance went well with his loquacity; but Emilio vouchsafed only a monosyllable in reply, something between a bark and grunt. 'How taciturn he is,' Lavinia thought. 'I will draw him out; I will practise my Italian on him; I will ask for information. *Questo?*' she demanded, indicating a sombre pile on the left. 'Palazzo Rezzonico,' he replied, speaking as though the name were heaven-sent, the explosive double z's so tamed and softened they might have fallen from the lips of an angel. 'That hasn't got us much further,' reflected Lavinia. 'Why does my vocabulary shrivel up directly I have a chance to use it? If the man had been an Eskimo I could have put the question in perfect Italian, using the feminine third person singular and all the apparatus of politeness. But one relapses into inarticulateness directly there is a risk of being understood. And come to that,' Lavinia pondered, frowning at the arabesque of scorpions and centipedes embroidered diagonally up her mother's dress, 'do I ever say what I mean when there is a likelihood of being understood? Perhaps it is fortunate that the likelihood is rare.' Association of ideas recalled Stephen Seleucis and his impending visit. 'If only, in thought, I could bring myself to call him "Ste",' she mused, 'perhaps I could oblige him and Mother. He cares for culture.'

Oi!

The sudden bellow startled her. Could Emilio have been responsible for it? She glanced up; he was staring impassive and unmoved, much as the campanile must stand after the frightful fracas of its striking midnight. They had left the Grand Canal behind and were elbowing their way up a narrow waterway; gone was all chance of seeing the Rialto, the object of their ride. No doubt Mrs Johnstone had noticed it. 'But really,' Lavinia reproached herself, 'I must do what I set out to do; otherwise I shall fall a prey to that anaemia of the will of which my Venetian compatriots so energetically boast. I shall consider my time wasted until I have satisfied myself whether Ruskin is right. Mamma thinks he is because her judgments follow her beliefs; my beliefs, if I could entertain any, would follow my judgments, if I could be certain what they were.'

Bui!

That was a good one, and a collision at this perilous corner providentially averted. Emilio and the coal man, *carboniere*, or whatever it is, have words, but without much ill-feeling, to judge from their faces. Emilio would look cross at any time, or is it savage, perhaps, or just stern, incorruptible, fearless, conscious of his Northern blood? He must be descended from the Visigoths I suppose; hence the colouring. How wonderfully he manages the gondola, taking it round these corners as cleanly as if it had a bend in its back. And here we are at the hotel.

The Splendid and Royal came into view, blinking behind its sun-blinds; and the servants, seeing with whom they had to deal, formed a circle on the steps, advertising their anxiety that Mrs Johnstone should make a successful landing. Even Emilio came down into the hold to give her his arm, stretching it out stiff at an odd impersonal angle, as though it was a bit of ship's furniture. The strength of her clasp left upon his skin a milky stain which faded even as Lavinia, bowed with books and rugs, momentarily laid her hand there. How cool it was, with all that sunshine stored up in it. She heard her mother's voice, raised to the pitch of indignant non-comprehension that had served her so well in life.

'Emilio wants, Emilio who?'

'Emilio Varagnolo, Madam, your gondolier.'

'Well, and what does he want?'

'He wants to be paid.'

'Lavinia,' said her mother, 'you're always wool-gathering. Here, give him this.'

But 'this', in all its eloquent parsimony, with all its air of making the foreigner, in his own territory, pay, was precisely what Lavinia could not give him. Already she had suffered much from those uncomfortable partings, from those muttered curses and black looks which were the certain outcome of giving Italians nothing but their due. In this case, it was less than what was due. Mrs Johnstone's blameless desire that people should not get the better of her generally ended, Lavinia knew, in her getting the better of them. Wondering by how much she should increase the fare she looked across and met the eyes of the gondolier, which also seemed to wonder. Hastily she pulled some notes out and, scarcely stopping to count them, walked down the little gangway and put them into his outstretched hand. What she had neglected to do, he did most thoroughly. With an absorption that might have amused her he reckoned up the sum, and, finding it tally with his expectations, or perhaps even rise to his hopes, he acknowledged her generosity with a dazzling smile and a magnificent salute. All the vitality of which she had been conscious, and whose application to alien activities she had vaguely resented, was suddenly released, let loose upon her in a flood. She shivered and turned away, only to be recalled.

'Madam! *Signorina*!'

'What is it?' Lavinia asked.

'Emilio wants to know if he shall return in the afternoon.' Instead of answering, Lavinia walked back to the steps. Emilio still wore his smile.

'*Venga qui alle due, alle due e mezzo*,' she said.

'*Va bene, Signorina*,' he answered, and was gone.

2

'I told the gondolier to come at half-past two,' Lavinia casually mentioned to her mother at luncheon.

'What gondolier, dear?' asked Mrs Johnstone.

'The one we had this morning.'

'Well, we don't want to encourage the man.'

'How do you mean, "encourage", Mamma?' Lavinia mildly enquired.

'I mean what I say,' said Mrs Johnstone without attempting further elucidation.

'Then,' pursued Lavinia, 'we shall be able to see La Madonna dell' Orto and all those churches on the Northern fringe.'

'Which day are they for?' demanded Mrs Johnstone, suspicion leaping into her voice.

'They are not all for a day,' confessed Lavinia, reluctantly admitting the inferior status of the churches on the Northern fringe. 'Tourists often neglect Sant' Alvise, though it is a gem and well repays a visit, the guide book says.'

'We are not tourists, whatever it may be,' remarked Mrs Johnstone.

'And,' continued Lavinia, momentarily elated by the success of her ruse, 'it contains the pseudo-Carpaccios, a notable instance, Mr Arrantoff says, of Ruskin's faulty *a priori* method and want of true critical sense.'

'Then I am sure I don't want to see them,' Mrs Johnstone declared. 'And who is Mr Arrantoff, anyhow?'

'He is quite modern,' said Lavinia feebly.

'All the more reason that he should be wrong,' her mother asserted. 'Ruskin was nearer Carpaccio's date, wasn't he?' [2]

'He wasn't contemporary,' said Lavinia.

'Perhaps not, but no doubt he had the tradition,' Mrs Johnstone retorted. 'In most cases, as you have told me more times than I can count, the tradition is all we have to go on. Ruskin went on it, I go on it, and you will, if you are sensible. But I am afraid sense is not your strong point, Lavinia. There's something I want to talk to you about. Remind me.'

'Can't you talk to me about it now?' Lavinia asked.

'I don't want everyone in the room to hear me,' her mother replied, raising her voice as though to justify her misgivings. Several people at neighbouring tables turned round in surprise. 'You see,' Mrs Johnstone commented complacently, 'I was right. They can hear. It will do in the gondola.'

They parted; Mrs Johnstone to rest, Lavinia to read. The first four volumes of Richardson's masterpiece[3] had yielded little but irritation. Why, she had asked herself a hundred times, if Clarissa really wanted to leave Lovelace, didn't she go? She wasn't a prisoner, but on she stayed, groaning, complaining, fainting, making scenes, when she might have walked out of the front door any hour in the twenty-four. Instead of which she tried to match her wits against the contrivances of a cad, hoping ultimately to charm him into a respectable citizen. But today Lavinia found herself more tolerant of Clarissa's voluntary bondage. Where, after all, could Miss Harlowe have gone? Would it be an agreeable home-coming for her, Lavinia, if after a parallel behaviour and a parallel experience she returned to the parental roof? Mrs Johnstone was not usually tender towards animals, but surely, on that occasion, she could be counted upon to spare the life of the fatted calf. 'Never, my dear Lavinia,' she affectionately admonished herself, 'let any situation get the upper hand of you.' She sighed, realising from past experience how improbable it was that any situation would put itself to the trouble. 'Not that I should welcome it,' she added, in an access of distaste. 'No Lovelaces for me.' She took up her coffee, which was growing cold, and looking over the brim of the cup she saw Emilio. He had arrived long before his time and was sitting on the low, carved chair, a luxury found only in the best gondolas, reading a newspaper. She watched his hands moving among the sheets, opening and closing. The thought that he could read gave her pleasure, such pleasure as might come from observing an unlooked-for accomplishment in one's own child. She wished he would lean back against the cushions and make himself comfortable: after all, it was his gondola. They cost seven thousand lire, a large sum for a poor man; and yet, as people who keep lodgings must let their best rooms to strangers and live in holes and corners themselves, so he, perhaps, had a scruple about taking the easiest seat. Warm and seductive, an humanitarian mood was visiting her, when the gondolier folded his paper, glanced up, and saw her. His face, she fancied, was friendly behind its glitter, he waved his hat and made a pretty show of activity; but when, in some confusion, she signed to him that she was not ready, he settled down to his paper again. Lavinia also returned to her book, but what she read did not hold her attention; the fact that she knew how to read didn't provide her with a solace, nor Emilio, to judge from his abstraction, with food for pleasurable thought. The dumb show in which she had taken part a moment since repeated itself before the ready auditorium of her mind; she saw his face alight with recognition; she tried to visualise his expression, penetrating, impatient, interrogatory, expectant. He looked as though any moment you might do something that would delight him. Why had she not done it? And yet what could she have done? She had an uneasy feeling that in the exchange of gestures she had not acquitted herself as she should have done, had missed an opportunity. 'Perhaps I can repair the error,' she thought, moving to a chair directly opposite the gondola. A smile rewarded her and she saw to it that this time her own greeting should not lack warmth.

3

Difficult to get at, more difficult to get into, infested outside by noisy children thirsting for money, and inside by sacristans more silent, but no less avaricious, the churches on the Northern fringe were everything that Lavinia had hoped. The September sunshine turned pink into rose, grey into green, danced reflected on the undersides of bridges and lent a healing touch to the cold rococo splendour of the Gesuiti, roofed and walled in gold. Devils at close quarters, at a distance the children with their ash-gold hair looked like angels taken from Bellini's pictures[4]. 'Don't give them anything,' Mrs Johnstone warned Lavinia, 'we must not encourage beggars.' '*Via, via,*' cried Lavinia, but they only mocked her, repeating the word in high glee, crowding round and pulling at her empty hands till her rings hurt her fingers. Even Emilio, rising in wrath on the poop and fixing them with a glare of unrestrained ferocity, scarcely quelled them. But he was a great help when anything went wrong, when a key couldn't be found, or when a church was hidden round a corner. Personal investigation, poking about on her own, was unthinkable to Mrs Johnstone. The unknown alarmed her and she never paused to think how she, in her turn, would have alarmed the unknown.

Standing all billowy and large, within a few feet of the fondamenta, she would majestically wave her parasol to Emilio, who, leaving the gondola in charge of a beggar, leapt to do her bidding. Not a single detail of his alacrity was lost upon Lavinia. She wondered how he could walk at all, above all how he could walk so fast; she imagined he would go lop-sided, twisted by the unequal exercise of his profession. But his coming ashore renewed her confidence, she liked to see him striding ahead, and she caught herself abetting her mother in her passion for guidance, even when such guidance clearly was not required.

Never had she felt happier than when, late in the afternoon, they left San Giobbe homeward bound. Or more conscious of virtue. Always a conscientious but rarely an ecstatic sightseer, she had presented to each picture, each sculpture, each tomb, a vitality as persistent as its own. She felt at one with Art. She discriminated, she had her favourites, but her sensibility remained keen and unwearied, never missing an aesthetic intention or misjudging its effectiveness. To what could she attribute this blissful condition? Lavinia did not know, but irrelevantly she turned round and asked the gondolier the name of a church they were passing. 'He will take me for an idiot,' she thought, 'for I have asked him once already.' 'Santa Maria dei Miracoli,' he informed her without a trace of impatience. Lavinia knew it, but she wanted to hear him say it; and she continued to look back at the receding edifice, long after its outlines had been eclipsed and replaced by the figure of Emilio.

Mrs Johnstone's voice, always startling, made her positively jump.

'Lavinia!'

'Yes, Mamma.'

Mrs Johnstone generally called her daughter to attention before speaking.

'It was about Ste Seleucis.'

'I knew it was,' Lavinia replied.

'Then why didn't you remind me?' her mother demanded. 'I might easily have forgotten.'

Lavinia was silent.

'Now, when he comes, I want you to be particularly nice to him.'

'I always am, Mamma; that's what he complains of,' Lavinia rejoined.

'Then you must cut the nice part out. Now there were four men in America you might have married, and their names were –'

'I could only have married one,' Lavinia objected.

'Their names were,' Mrs Johnstone pursued, 'Stephen Seleucis, Theodore Drakenburg, Michael B. Sprott, and Walt Watt. They were not good enough for you.' Mrs Johnstone paused to let this sink in. 'What did they do? They married someone else.'

'Three other people in all,' Lavinia amended.

'But Stephen didn't,' said Mrs Johnstone, as though virtue disclaimed the abbreviation that affection craved. 'And next week, I hope you will give him a different answer.'

Lavinia looked upwards at the Bridge of Sighs. 'I should be very inconsistent if I did,' she said at last.

'Who wants you to be consistent?' asked Mrs Johnstone. 'When you are married you can be as consistent as you like. But not when you are turned twenty-seven and unmarried, and have a grey hair or two, and the reputation of being as forbidding to decent men as the inside of Sing-Sing prison[5]. I could say more, but I will refrain, because you are my daughter and I don't want to hurt your feelings.'

A confession of belated solicitude always rounded off Mrs Johnstone's harangues on this topic; it had become a formula.

'Decent men?' Lavinia echoed, watching the throng of loungers on the piazzetta. 'You don't think it's their decency that makes me dislike them?' She spoke without irony, reflectively.

'Well, I don't know what else you had to find fault with,' remarked Mrs Johnstone, 'except their looks. Ste isn't a beauty; but you can't have everything.'

'I am content to have nothing,' muttered Lavinia. In the fuss of landing, for they had reached the hotel, her rebellious utterance escaped censure. Disencumbered, her mother trod heavily upon the fragile gangway, to disappear amid solicitous servants. She herself remained to collect their traps, hidden by the gathering dusk. Some had slipped off Mrs Johnstone as she rose, her amplitude, as a watershed for these trifles, making the range of search wide, almost incalculable. She knelt, she groped. 'I *will* find them,' thought Lavinia, and then, as her hand closed upon the last, 'why should I find them?' She replaced her mother's smelling-bottle in a crevice of the cushions, and appealed to Emilio with a gesture of despair. Instantly he was on his knees beside her. The search lasted for a full minute. Then '*Ecco, ecco,*' cried the gondolier, delighted by his discovery, holding the smelling-bottle as tenderly as if it had been the relic of a saint. Infected by his high spirits, exalted into a mood she did not recognise, Lavinia stretched out her hand for the bottle and smiled into his eyes. Their exquisite mockery, the overtone of their glitter, annihilated time. Lavinia passed beyond thought into a stellar region where all sensations were one. Then the innumerable demands of life swarmed back and settled upon her, dealing their tiny stings. For one thing Emilio must be paid.

But Emilio had no change. He searched himself, he turned this way and that; he bent forward as though wounded, and backward as though victorious. His hands apologised, his face expressed concern, but not a lira could he find to dilute Lavinia's fifty. So she gave him the note, and then followed the incident which was eventually to cause her much distress and self-reproach. That she didn't, at the time, divine its importance the casual entry in her diary shows.

*The depression I have felt the last few weeks left me today; why, I cannot think. Perhaps the homily I gave myself last night in bed has borne fruit. I resolved not to be idle, discontented or inattentive, but to throw myself into life and let the current carry me whither it would. Nothing of the sort seems to have happened; I haven't taken any plunge; but this morning, on the Grand Canal, and still more this afternoon, going round the churches with Mamma (how that bored me at Verona, see August 30th and resolution), I felt extraordinarily happy. (*Here the words, *Perhaps I have a capacity for happiness after all,* were deleted.*) Not quite so happy after dinner when we went out to listen to the piccola serenata; that was with a different gondolier. I think I shall persuade Mamma to stick to the one we had this afternoon, engage him by the day. He wanted to come for us this evening, and I have asked myself since (although it is a trivial matter) why I said we shouldn't need him. I should be sorry if he thought us ungrateful for all his help, but I felt, just at the moment, that I had overpaid him and it would be disagreeable, with the same man, to reduce the rate in future; also I wasn't sure whether Mamma might not prefer the Piazza, and then he would be disappointed of his fare. I don't want to appear capricious. Emilio didn't take my saying no very well, not as pleasantly as he took my fifty-lire note; I thought he scowled at me, but it was almost too dark to see. What does it matter? but he had been charming, and it is so seldom a foreigner takes a genuine interest in one. I hope I wasn't mean over the money; but it makes it hard for poorer people if you give too much, and isn't really good for the*

Italians themselves. It would be a pity to spoil Emilio. How lovely the false Carpaccios were – I prefer them to the real ones. Is there anything else? Hiding the smelling-bottle wasn't the same thing as a lie – just a game, like hunt-the-thimble.

4

Every prospect in Venice gives the beholder a sense of unworthiness and of being born out of time; but Lavinia, arrived early on the terrace next morning, was scarcely at all conscious of inferiority. The sun was brilliant, the water as still as it would ever be. Incompatibilities did not trouble her. The great American cruiser moored at the side of the Bacino, leaning against the land, reassured her by its stability; the Trieste liner, stealthily revolving on itself, contrasted pleasantly with the small fry that looked purposeless and stationary, but were no doubt working hard to get out of the monster's way. The island of St Giorgio was evidently the work of a magician; every building fitted into the *cliché* that guide-books and tourists had agreed upon for it. 'The Salute itself,' thought Lavinia, looking her ancient enemy squarely in the face, 'has a decorative quality, and decoration is something, though of course not the essence of art. Even that ruffianly-looking gondolier is improved by his crimson sash. Now if Emilio had one –' And pat to her thought Emilio appeared, cleaving his way towards her and dressed, not in the dingy weeds of yesterday, but in a white suit with a sky-blue scarf that lay like a lake upon his chest, and a sash that poured itself away in a cascade of flounces from the knot at his side.

Lavinia made up her mind quickly. Espying a high functionary she took her courage in both hands and addressed him. 'Could she engage Emilio as Mrs Johnstone's private gondolier?'

The man's manner, a disagreeable blend of insolence and servility, grew oilier and more offensive.

'No, you cannot have him, he is already engaged; the lady

and gentleman who went out with him last night have taken him from day to day.'

'Oh,' said Lavinia, suddenly listless. So this was the meaning of the fine apparel, the meaning of the gondola encrusted with gilt and dripping with fringes? She had been forestalled. Her eyes travelled over the sumptuous vessel and Emilio made her a little salute – the acknowledgement due to a late employer – without much heart in it. She could not go on standing where she was. Despondent she walked back to her chair. The balcony had become a cage, and the day was brilliant, she felt, in spite of her.

'Lavinia!'

'Yes, Mamma.'

'You don't look as though you had slept any too well. Did you?' Tenderness and interest alike were absent from Mrs Johnstone's enquiry; its tone suggested both certainty and disapproval, and she went on, without waiting for a reply:

'But I've got some good news for you, or what ought to be good news. I give you three guesses.'

Now play up, Lavinia.

'The worldly Elizabeth Templeman is coming here from Rome?'

'Wrong. She is still in bed with the chill she so foolishly caught wandering about the Coliseum after nightfall.'

'The exchange?'

'The exchange is two points worse. Really, Lavinia, you should know these things.' Mrs Johnstone could make even guessing dangerous.

'Then it must be that Stephen isn't –'

'Isn't! Is, and Monday too. With the Evanses. Now I ought to tell you that Amelia Fielder Evans –'

'My rival?'

'Amelia Fielder Evans,' said Mrs Johnstone warningly, 'is a very determined woman.'

'Yes,' sighed Lavinia. 'He certainly should be saved from her.'

'Well, you can save him,' Mrs Johnstone observed, 'and you can do it at dinner on Tuesday. Amelia will be tired from her journey. Now what?'

'Should we bathe?' suggested Lavinia.

'Heavens! But I thought you wanted to go in a gondola. You are changeable, Lavinia.'

'You have always wanted to see the Lido, Mamma.'

'Very well, then.'

'We'll walk to the vaporetto. It's not far.'

Off they went.

5

How brief is human happiness, Lavinia wrote that night in her diary. *My exaltation of yesterday has almost passed away. I loathed the Lido: all those khaki-coloured bodies lying about, half-interred in sand or sprawling over bridge tables, disgusted me inexpressibly. My Puritan blood stirred within me. Why must they make themselves so common? The people who hired our gondolier came out in the afternoon; they were among the worst, perfectly shameless. Mamma was surprised when I went up to speak to them, but one must be civil to people staying in the same hotel. You never know what you may want from them, as Elizabeth Templeman would say. When they heard who we were, they were impressed and showed it; they come from Pittsburgh, their speech bewrayeth them. They offered to take us in their gondola whenever we liked. Mamma was for refusing and reproached me afterwards because I said we would. But are we not all God's people? We live too much in a groove, and personalities are more interesting than places, as I have proved in many an essay. Still, even as they left my lips, the gracious words of consent surprised me. Strangers are my abhorrence and my instinct was to dislike these, with their name like a Greek toothpaste, Kolynopulo. America is a nation of hyphens and hybrids.*

How discontented all this sounds. I must make a resolution against exclusiveness, a besetting sin. I have always meant to visit the poor, but Venice is not a good place to begin in... How it would surprise Emilio if I turned up at his home, bringing a tract against profanity! The churches are plastered with notices begging the people not to disgrace the glorious language of Dante, Alfieri, Petrarch, etc. I have an idea what his home is like: it would be fun to see if it is a true one!

6

'Shame your mother couldn't come,' said Mr Kolynopulo, assisting Lavinia, with more gallantry than was necessary, into his gorgeous gondola. 'Does she often have headaches?'

Miss Johnstone wore a harassed air. 'Venice doesn't really suit her,' she replied. 'It's the tiresome sirocco.' She looked wistfully down the lagoon to where that climatic nuisance was wont to assert its presence with an unanswerable visibility; but the air had lost its fever, could not have been clearer. 'The very heavens give me the lie,' she thought; and aloud she said, 'Oh! no, Mr Kolynopulo, you must let me be selfish and sit here.' To clinch the argument she sank into the half-way seat. 'Venice depends so much on where you sit. Here I can see forwards and sideways and even backwards.' Suiting the action to the word, she gazed earnestly at a point directly in their wake; her scrutiny also included Emilio, who did not return it, but stared angrily at the horizon.

'Good-looking, isn't he?' remarked Mrs Kolynopulo, indicating Emilio with her thumb.

Lavinia started.

'I suppose he is. I never thought about it,' she said.

'Then you're different from most,' Mrs Kolynopulo answered. 'I guess he's caused a flutter in many a female breast. We considered ourselves lucky to get him. We've been the subject of congratulation.'

'Not from me,' thought Lavinia, eyeing congratulation's twin subjects with ill-concealed distaste.

'Do you share the flutter?' she presently enquired.

'Bless you, no,' replied his wife. 'We're married. We leave that sort of thing to the single ones.'

The slaves of matrimony exchanged affectionate looks and

even, to Lavinia's horror, kissed each other. She wanted to let the subject drop, but instead she asked:

'What sort of thing?'

'What sort of thing which, dear?' Mrs Kolynopulo playfully asked her.

'What sort of thing do you… leave?' said Lavinia, with an effort making her meaning clear.

Her temporary hosts looked archly at each other, then laughed long and loud.

'My dear!' protested Mrs Kolynopulo, still quivering like a jelly.

'You forget, my pretty,' her husband reproved her, 'that Miss Johnstone has been properly brought up.'

'Oh dear, you Boston girls, you ingénues!' Mrs Kolynopulo sighed. 'Ask us another time.'

But Lavinia had had a revulsion. 'May my tongue rot if I do,' she thought, and to change the subject she asked their immediate destination.

'To see the glass made,' Mr Kolynopulo replied. 'Venetian glass, what?'

'Yes, Venetian, of course,' Lavinia repeated helplessly.

'Well, isn't it one of the recognised sights? We've seen the prison and the pigeons.'

'Oh, perfectly recognised,' Lavinia almost too heartily agreed. 'I see the posters and the man with the leaflets.'

They disembarked.

7

On their return they found Mrs Johnstone seated under an awning, a rug across her knees, a bitter-looking cordial at her elbow. The chair beside her was occupied by a mound of American newspapers, and in front of her another chair supported her work – a box of silks and a vast oval frame within which the features of a sylvan scene had begun to disclose themselves. A pale green fountain rose into the air, whose jet, symmetrically bifurcated, played upon a formal cluster of lambs in one corner and a rose-red rock in the other.

The Kolynopulos approached as near as the barricade permitted. Mrs Johnstone did not dismantle it, nor did she rise.

'I'm glad you took Lavinia to the glass-factory,' she observed, when the conventional expressions of sympathy had exhausted themselves. 'I could never get her to go. She won't take any interest in trade processes, though I often ask her where she'd be without them.'

'We should still have each other,' said Lavinia.

'Of course we should, darling,' Mrs Johnstone remarked, greatly pleased. 'What more do we want?' The question hung in the air until the retirement of the Kolynopulos, bowing and smiling, seemed to have answered it.

'Oh, Mamma,' said Lavinia, much concerned. 'I did not know you were ill.'

'You might have done,' her mother replied. 'I told you.'

'Yes,' conceded Lavinia, 'but –'

'You are right in a way,' admitted Mrs Johnstone. 'It came on afterwards. Providence would not have me a liar. All the same, I don't like your new friends, Lavinia.'

'Nor do I, altogether,' Lavinia confessed.

'Then why let them take you out?'

'Well, we can't both have headaches, for our own sakes,' Lavinia obscurely replied.

'It's not necessary to have them more than once, and mine could have served for both of us, if you'd let it,' Mrs Johnstone answered. 'You don't understand, Lavinia. Undesirable acquaintances may be kept off in a variety of ways. You saw how I did it just now.'

'But that was very crude, Mamma, you must own, and may have wounded them.'

'If so, I shall have struck oil.' Mrs Johnstone paused to appreciate her joke. 'No; it's like this. You cannot be too careful. Our station in life is associated with a certain point of view and a certain standard of conduct. Once you get outside it, anything may happen to you. People like that may easily put ideas into your head, and then it'll be no good coming to me to get them out.'

'Would it be any good going to them?' In vision Lavinia saw her mind as an aquarium, in which a couple of unattractive minnows, the gift of the Kolynopulos, eluded Mrs Johnstone's unpractised hand.

'You'd probably find them more sympathetic,' her mother replied. 'But they couldn't help you, any more than you can help me to get rid of this chill, though you may be said to have given it me, since I caught it bathing with you. But I think you might stay in this afternoon and try.'

After luncheon Lavinia excused herself from accompanying the Kolynopulos on their visit to the Arsenal.

In her diary she wrote:

Poor Mamma, she hasn't the least notion of what is meant by individualism. She has read Emerson because he was a connection of ours; but she won't cast her bantling on the rocks, as he advised.[6] *The Kolynopulos may be carelessly moulded, they are certainly not rough hewn, and they are well above the surface; indeed, they set out to attract all eyes; it would be a silly ship that went aground on them. How can it make any difference to one's soul, that inviolable entity, whom one meets? Milton could not praise a fugitive and cloistered virtue.*[7] *I welcome whatever little trials the Ks. see fit to put mine to. I have summed them up; I know their tricks and their manners; I can look after myself. When their conversation becomes disagreeable, I can always change the subject, as I did this morning. They thought they were working upon my curiosity, whereas all the time I was leading them on. But, to be quite honest (though why I should say that I don't know, since this diary is a record of my most intimate thoughts) I wouldn't have gone with them, but for Emilio. What a contrast he is to them. No wonder people congratulated them, as they might congratulate a toad on its jewel. It must be irksome for him to propel such people about. I hope he distinguishes between us; I hope he knows I only go in their gondola on his account. Do I really want him to know that? Perhaps not; but if you like anyone you can't rest till they know you like them. I didn't realise I liked him until Mrs Kolynopulo said everyone did; then I saw that they must, and the thought gave me great pleasure. I believe I could stay in Venice for ever. Certainly when the Ks. depart (which is in five days now) I shall engage him. And so to bed, 'pillowed on a pleasure', to quote Mr Myers.*[8]

Monday. – *I am a little uneasy about Mamma. If I hadn't gone to Torcello (and it takes the best part of the day by gondola) she would have stayed in. She didn't want me to go, and perhaps I ought not to have gone; it is dull for her being alone; but she needn't feel so strongly about the Kolynopulos: they are quite amusing in their way, and she might just as well have come with us. Now she has a temperature again, nothing much. I offered to sit up with her the first part of the night, but she wouldn't hear of it. Too late for the Evanses and Stephen to call now; I am glad, rather, that they couldn't get rooms at this hotel. Another scene with Mamma about Stephen. She thinks that if I don't marry him I'll never marry anyone; it is hard for us to make new friends, the choice is so small. The proximity of Amelia goads her into saying more than she means. I told her that Stephen meant nothing to me; since I had been at Venice he had ceased to exist for me. She asked why Venice had made any difference. I couldn't tell her about Emilio, who is the real reason – not that I am in love with him – Heavens! but my thoughts turn on him in a special way; they run on oiled wheels, and if I try to think about Stephen at the same time the reverie breaks up, most painfully. I owe Stephen nothing. He lectures me and domineers over me and the sight of him recalls scenes of my childhood I would much rather forget. The fact that he has loved me for ten years only exasperates me; it is a thought outside my scheme, I don't know how to deal with it. Sufficient unto the day: tomorrow will settle all. Pray heaven he may have fallen in love with Amelia.*

8

But he hadn't. Lavinia found him, when she came down next morning, sitting in an arm-chair which he scarcely seemed to touch, poring over a map. He had been waiting an hour, he said, and had already seen her mother, who was much better.

'Yes, a good deal better,' said Lavinia, who had also seen her.

'Very much better,' he repeated, as though the information, coming from his lips, had a peculiar authenticity. 'And now as to plans,' he continued. 'I have worked out two programmes for the next five days – one for Mr and Mrs Evans and Amelia, and your mother, if she is well enough to go with them; they don't know Venice. Another, more advanced itinerary for us. Just look here.' He summoned her to the map, and Lavinia, feeling like a map herself, all signs and no substance, complied; but not without a feeble protest.

'But I don't know Venice either.'

'Ah, but you are intelligent, you can learn,' he said. Lavinia resented everything in his remark; the implication that her mother was not intelligent, the readiness to agree that she herself was quick but ignorant.

'I don't know which end the map is up,' she said suddenly.

'What! Not know your compass? We shall have to begin further back than I thought. Now, you're the North. I'll set the map by you. Here is the Piazza: do you see?'

'Yes,' said Lavinia.

'Well, where?'

Lavinia pointed to it.

'Right. Now I've drawn a series of concentric circles, marking on them everything we've got to see. I don't count tourists' tit-bits, like Colleoni and the Frari.'

'I love equestrian statues,' declared Lavinia. 'There are only sixty-four, I believe, in the world. And the Pesaro Madonna is almost my favourite picture in Venice.'

'Well,' said Stephen, 'we'll see what time we've got. Now here's the first circle of our inferno. What do you put on it? Remember, you've been here nearly a week.' He turned towards Lavinia an acute questioning glance; a pedagogue's glance. His brows were knitted under his thin straight hair; his large prominent features seemed to start from his face and make a dent on Lavinia's mind. Not a mist, not a shadow of diffidence in his impatient eyes; no slightest preoccupation with her or with himself, only an unabashed anxiety to hear her answer. Lavinia resolved it should be as wrong as she could possibly make it.

'St Francesco della Vigna,' she suggested, putting her head on one side, a gesture that ordinarily she loathed beyond all others.

He looked at her in consternation; then let the map fall to his knees.

'Why, Lavinia,' he exclaimed. 'You're not trying.'

Tears of mortification came into her eyes.

'I don't think I want to learn,' she confessed.

'Why, of course you don't,' he replied, relieved by this simple explanation of her contumacy. 'No one does. But we've got to. That's what we Americans come here for. Now, try again.'

'Perhaps I could do better outside,' Lavinia temporised. The terrace revealed the Canal, and the Canal, Emilio. He was leaning against a post, expending, it seemed, considerable energy, for the prow of the gondola swung rapidly round. But whatever the exertion, he absorbed it into himself. The economy of movement was complete. There were no ineffective gestures, no effort run to waste; a thousand years of

35

watermanship were expressed in that one manoeuvre. The gondolier saw Lavinia, took off his black hat, and smiled as he draped himself across his platform. There he sat. He smiled when you smiled, generally. He took you where you wanted to go. He forced nothing upon you. He demanded nothing of you. He had no questions, he had no replies. At every moment he was accessible to pleasure; at every moment, unconsciously, he could render pleasure back; it lived in his face, his movements, his whole air, where all the charms of childhood, youth and maturity mingled without losing their identity.

'There's a good-looking man if you like,' Lavinia's companion remarked.

'Yes, he's considered good-looking,' Lavinia concurred.

'I call him very good-looking,' Stephen repeated, as though there was nothing beautiful or ugly but his thinking made it so.

9

'No,' said Miss Evans, speaking, it seemed, for the first time that evening. 'We shall not stay long in Venice.' She rose and stretched herself.

They were sitting, all of them, in the Piazza. Dinner had been a failure, and its sequel, though enlivened by a band and a continual recourse to Florian's refreshments, a disaster.

'Bed-time?' muttered Mr Evans, brushing his waistcoat with his hands. He jingled his watch-chain which had retained flakes of ash, uncertain in which direction gravity, such was the ambiguity of gradient on Mr Evans's waistcoat, meant them to go.

'If Amelia wishes,' his wife primly replied.

'I do,' said Amelia.

They parted, Stephen accompanying Lavinia and her mother to their hotel.

'You must take care of that cold, Mrs. Johnstone,' he said, as they stopped at the door. 'And will you lend me Lavinia for half-an-hour? I want her to see the Rialto by moonlight.'

'I always do one or two things for Mother before she goes to bed,' Lavinia protested.

'Am I quite helpless?' demanded Mrs Johnstone. 'Am I utterly infirm? You make me feel an old woman, Lavinia, fussing about after me. Take her, Ste, by all means.'

Lavinia was taken.

On the fondamenta, below the Rialto, they encountered an émeute. Cries rang out; there was a scuffle in which blows were exchanged and blood flowed. Terrified by the sight of men bent on hurting each other, Lavinia tried to draw Stephen away, but he detained her, showing a technical interest in the methods of the combatants.

'Your real Italian,' he said, mimicking the action, 'always stabs from underneath, like this.'

Panic seized Lavinia. She felt vulnerable all over. The malignant light of the moon served only to reveal shadows and darkness; darkness under the great span of the Rialto, darkness in the thick foliage that shrouded the Casa Petrarca, darkness in the antic figures which tripped and rose and struggled with each other in the sheet of pale light that carpeted the fondamenta.

At last Stephen yielded to her entreaties.

'Well, I'm glad I saw that,' he said. But Lavinia felt that something alien, some quality of the night, had entered into her idea of Venice and would persist even in the noonday glare. It was to Stephen she owed this illumination, or rather this obfuscation, and she could not forgive him.

The narrowness of the *mercerie*[9] brought them close together.

'Lavinia,' he said, 'I'm going to ask you a question. I suppose you know what it is.'

She did know, and her unwillingness to hear was aggravated tenfold by his obtuseness in choosing the moment when she liked him less than she had ever done. She was silent.

'Don't you know? Well, what should I be likely to ask?'

Lavinia trembled with obstinacy and rage.

'Well now,' he said, with the air of giving her an easier one. 'What do I generally ask?' He pressed her arm; a thrill of hysteria ran through her. 'Put it another way,' he said. 'In your small but sometimes valuable opinion, Lavinia, what am I most in need of?'

Lavinia's self-control deserted her.

'Consideration, imagination, everything except self-confidence,' she said, and burst into tears.

They walked in silence across the piazza, in silence past St Moses to Lavinia's hotel.

'Good-night,' he said. There were tears in his voice, and she hated him for that. 'I didn't know you disliked me, Lavinia. I will go away tomorrow, to Verona, I think. Bless you.'

He was gone. Lavinia listened at her mother's door; no sound. She went to bed but her thoughts troubled her, and at about a quarter to four she rose and took out her diary.

I could never have married Stephen, but I didn't mean to be cruel to him, she wrote. *I don't know what came over me. At the time there seemed nothing else to say; but on reflection I can think of a dozen things I might have said, all without wounding him. And he has such deep feelings, like most unselfconscious people, whose interest in a subject blinds them to the fact that they may be boring others with it. He really cares for me, and I ought to have been flattered by his enthusiasm and zeal for my improvement, instead of wanting him to let me go to the devil my own way. Is that where I am bound? I detected a whiff of brimstone this evening and I'm not sure whether this room is clear of it yet. I wasn't really angry with him; that's where he has the advantage over me; I was exasperated and unnerved, whereas he is now plunged, I fear, into real old-fashioned misery, the sort that keeps you awake at nights and is too hard and too heavy to yield to soft analysis. Well, I am awake, too. But that's because I worry about myself: I am so concerned with self-justification that I whittle away the shame I ought to feel, externalising it and nibbling bits off it until I grow interested and quite proud of it. If I had a proper nature, instead of this putty-soft putty-coloured affair, my relations towards people would fall into their right places,* and not need readjustment at the hands of my sensibility. No one knows where they are with me, because they really aren't anywhere; I am forever making up my mind about myself.

There, I have succeeded in my discreditable design: I feel easier. But that doesn't mean I am worse than those who don't know in what direction to aim their self-reproaches. Why should stupidity be held the mark of a fine nature? I am not the more bad because I realise where my badness lies. But I dread tomorrow, with Stephen going away hurt, the Evanses piqued, Mother unwell, and only the Kolynopulos to fall back on – and Emilio, of course. I had almost forgotten him.

Lavinia's misgivings were not unfounded. In the morning, still keeping her bed, Mrs Johnstone had an audience first of Stephen, then of the Evanses, and, finally, of her daughter, who had gone for refuge and solace to a hairdresser's, where she had let herself, half unwillingly, be the subject of successive and extremely time-taking remedial processes, each one imposed upon her with a peculiar affront. It was depressing, this recital of her hair's shortcomings; dry, brittle, under-nourished, split at the ends, it seemed only to stay on, as the buildings of Venice were said to stand, out of politeness. Ploughed, harrowed, sown and reaped, Lavinia's scalp felt like a battlefield. A proposal to exacerbate it further she resisted.

'Does Madam want to lose *all* her hair?'

'No, you idiot, of course I don't.'

Through a film of soapy water Lavinia's eyes tried to blaze; they smarted instead.

'I might just as well cry,' she thought, and seeing the woeful image in the mirror she shed a few tears which didn't show in the general mess.

She appeared before her mother with a false air of freshness.

'Who was it tired her head and was thrown out of a window?' asked Mrs Johnstone, glaring from the bed.

It is my lot to have to answer stupid questions, Lavinia thought.

'Jezebel,[10] that much-married woman,' she replied.

'Now that's where you're wrong,' Mrs Johnstone contradicted her. 'She married once; it was the only respectable thing she did.'

'The Psalms say she was all glorious within until she

married. Later it says, "So long as the whoredoms of thy mother Jezebel" – I forget what.'

'Lavinia!'

A long silence followed. Miss Johnstone, regardless of her prototype's defenestration, leaned out of the window. Her own bedroom opened on to an interior court: it must be pleasant to have a room with a view.[11]

'Lavinia,' said her mother at last, 'I don't think Venice is doing you any good. You've sent Ste away broken-hearted; you've offended the Evanses, you've made me ill; and now you address your own mother in the language of the market-place.'

'The language of the Bible,' interposed Lavinia.

'You'll go to the agency now and book places for us in the Orient express. We'll start tomorrow, or Friday at the latest.'

'The Wagons-Lits Company, like the churches,' said Lavinia, 'closes between twelve and two.' The impulse to profanity was new to her, and as she left her mother's room she regarded the intruder with dismay, an emotion soon overpowered by the realisation that in a few hours' time she would have to leave Venice. During her solitary luncheon she scoured her mind for a device to circumvent her marching-orders; all the way to the Piazza she asked herself, 'Is there no way out?' She could think of none.

It was the clerk at the counter who, all involuntarily, for he could never willingly have been helpful in his life, showed her the way.

'When do you want to go?' he said, when Lavinia, squashed, elbowed and pounded, at last reached him.

Lavinia pondered. She did not want to go at all. What was the effect, psychologically, of saying you wanted something that you passionately did not want? Did it do you any good? How did the will, thwarted, revenge itself? Where did its energy go, since it was incompressible and must find an outlet somewhere? It might assert itself in some very extravagant fashion. When she spoke, it was with her lips only.

'Tomorrow,' she said.

'You can't go tomorrow,' the man replied, his face lighting up with a joy that, contrasted with the ordinary cast of his features, seemed almost innocent.

Lavinia's lips moved again. She would give Providence its chance.

'Friday?'

'Full up, Friday,' said the man, again as though the congestion of the train afforded him immense satisfaction. 'But you can go –'

'Stop,' said Lavinia, running her fingers over the counter and pausing at the third finger of her right hand. 'Will you give me two tickets to Paris for Friday week?'

She walked back, as though in a dream, straight to her mother's room. All the petulance had gone from her manner, and she felt, as she saw Mrs Johnstone propped on the pillows, with so much that made her formidable either left out or undone, that she could wait upon her mother for ever.

'I am very sorry, Mamma,' she said, 'but all the sleeping-cars to Paris are reserved till next Friday week. So I took tickets for then. I hope you don't mind, and I think it's for the best; you really aren't fit to travel.'

'If I'm fit to stay here I'm fit for anything,' Mrs Johnstone replied. 'You're sure you went to the right place, Lavinia?'

'Certain, Mamma.'

'Well, I don't imagine it will be much pleasure for you to stay,' Mrs Johnstone remarked, as though Lavinia were a scapegoat for the sins of the railway company, and that was a comfort.

11

I never thought, Lavinia wrote that evening, *that one result of wrong-doing was to ease the temper. I feel like an angel. It is so long since I did anything I knew to be wrong, I had quite forgotten the taste of it. Certainly I must try again. To do wrong against one's will, as I did last night, how disagreeable! But with the full approval of conscience (it must have approved, or it wouldn't have let me be so nice to Mamma) how intoxicating! Before, when I felt I must only be good, my choice was confined, in fact I had no choice. Now, at last, I see the meaning of free will, which no one can see who has not wilfully done wrong. Even the people who say they always act for the best, and do so much harm, never get an inkling (it is their punishment) of the pleasure they would have if they knew, as others do, that they are really acting for the worst. The joys of hypocrisy are not self-sufficing, they depend upon the approval of others, whereas deliberate sin can be relished only by oneself; of all pleasures it is the least communicable. Why, I wonder, is that? Let me take an instance. Suppose I saw Emilio beating his mother, because his choice that day happened to be surfeited with good? He would be enjoying himself, just as I enjoyed prolonging our stay by deceiving my mother; but should I enjoy seeing him? Perhaps not, but then cruelty is a thing apart; no one can want to be cruel. Suppose I saw him kissing someone – someone he had no right to kiss? That wouldn't please me either. But if I saw him give alms to a beggar? That would delight me, I know, for I've often wished he would. Well, there's no moral to be drawn from this, except that one should keep one's wickedness within oneself; to look at it from outside seems to dim its lustre. I will not be the spectator of my own mother-beating. Self-examination looks askance upon forbidden delights and morbidity is a force making for righteousness: away with it.*

12

The regatta of Murano was a sorry affair. Even the Koly-nopulos, whose ready response to advertised spectacles had prompted the expedition, confessed disappointment. The dowdy little island was seething with people; the race was conducted with much fuss and continual clearing of the course; but when it actually happened, after a lapse of several hours, excitement had worn itself out and given way to impatience. No gondola, reflected Lavinia, as the first man home was received with shouts and pistol-shots, should ever try to suggest speed. It was like a parody of a boat race, the exhaustion of the performers remaining, the thrill left out, and an air of troubled and unnatural competition hanging over all. On their way back, at Lavinia's request, they visited St Francesco della Vigna. From across the lagoon the great Campanile had kept catching her eye, its shaft in the purple, its summit in the blue. She promised herself a moment of meditation in the melancholy cloister; but for some reason the church failed her. The ruinous shrine in the centre of the garth assumed a pagan look; the shadows were too thick for comfort; the darkness had nothing to tell her; the heavy doors were locked against her. She purposely outpaced Mrs Kolynopulo, whose eyes were long in accustoming themselves to the half-light, to seek out a column she remembered – a column which supported a creeper, common enough, and wispy and poor, but lovely from one's consciousness of its rarity in Venice. But its greenness had gone grey, its leaves were falling, and the defeated tendrils, clawing the air, symbolised and reaffirmed her failure to recapture the emotion of her first visit.

Leaving her companion behind, she hastened back to

the gondola. Mr Kolynopulo was asleep, sprawled across the cushions, his head over-weighting the hand that sought to sustain it. Emilio, also, was resting, but as she came he threw himself across the poop into an attitude that absurdly caricatured his fare's. Lavinia laughed and clapped her hands; gone was her sense of isolation, gone her wish to re-create herself by a sentimental communion with the past. The darkness, palpable and unnerving in the cloister, fell into its place, dwindled into a time of day, was absorbed by Emilio and forgotten. Something that had stirred and asserted itself at the back of her mind fell asleep, seemed to die, leaving her spirits free. She resolved to avail herself of a security, a superiority to circumstance, that might vanish as suddenly as it came.

'Mrs Kolynopulo,' she said, pronouncing the ridiculous name more seriously than ever before, 'you said I might ask you a question: do you remember?'

'No, dear; I can't say that I do.'

'It was about the gondoliers.' Lavinia's buoyancy remained, though she detected a wobble in her flight.

'What about them, dear?' Mrs Kolynopulo enquired.

Lavinia realised then that her difficulty in putting the question was in itself a partial answer to it; but she had gone too far to draw back.

'You said that married people did not – had not... certain... dealings with the gondoliers that unmarried people had. I wondered what you meant.'

'Why, you've got it, my dear,' Mrs Kolynopulo chuckled. 'You've said it yourself.'

A sensation of nausea came over Lavinia. She felt degraded and shown up, as though, in a first effort to steal, she had been caught red-handed by a pickpocket of older standing.

'*What* have I said?' she muttered. 'I haven't said anything.'

'Oh yes, you have,' her mentor rejoined. 'You said that certain people had dealings with gondoliers. Well, they do. Relations, it's generally called.'

'Why do they?' Lavinia murmured stupidly.

'Who, dear? The people, or the gondoliers?'

Oh, the agony of answering that question, the effort of bringing her mind to bear upon it. She turned the alternatives over and over, as though playing heads and tails with herself. The words began to have no meaning for her. At last she said:

'The gondoliers.'

'Well,' Mrs Kolynopulo answered in a tone of considerable relief, 'you may be sure they don't do it for nothing.'

Lavinia said not a word on the way home, and when she went to bed her diary remained unopened. She seemed to have become inarticulate, even to herself.

13

The following evening, however, she resumed her record.

I wish I could have left yesterday out of my life, as I left it out of my diary. I didn't mean to refer to it; indeed I didn't mean to add another word to this confession. It is false; it is a sham; there is a lie in every line of it. So, at least, I thought this morning. I have always been, and always shall be, the kind of character the last few days have proved me to be: I am the Lavinia who was cruel to Stephen, who snapped the head off a poor hairdresser, who shocked her mother with an indecent word, and imperilled her health with a lie, who worried two boon companions into disclosing a scandal as untrue as it was vile. This is the house Lavinia has built, and a proper pigsty it is; but real, quite real, unlike the decorous edifice whose pleasing lines are discernible in the pages of this diary and which is a fake, a fallacious façade with nothing behind it. I have lost the power to regulate my life; I feel as though it had suddenly grown too big for me; it fits only where it touches, and it touches only to hurt. I feel that all appeals that are made to me are sent to the wrong address. Lavinia Johnstone passed away early in the week and the person who wears her semblance is a very different creature, who would as soon spit in your eye as speak to you. It is a relief to talk of myself in the third person, I get rid of myself that way: if only I could isolate the new me, and enclose the intruder in a coffin of wax, as bees do! What distressed me in reading Elizabeth's letter this morning was to find that, already, I had ceased to respond to the touches which were meant for me as she knew me; they fell on a dead place. But it will be a long time before my friends notice the change, before I become as strange to them as I am already to myself! And, meanwhile, I can feed their affections with the embalmed Lavinia. It is not a disgusting thought: Mummy was once merchandise – Mizraim cured wounds – Pharaoh was sold for balsams.[12] *No doubt many people before me have had to meet the public demand for versions of themselves which, though out of date and superseded, please better than their contemporary personalities could hope to do.*

14

At last the Kolynopulos had gone; gone without leaving Lavinia the reversion of their gondolier. All day she had struggled to put her plea before them; a hundred times she had changed the wording of her request. Elaborately casual it would have to be; she would breathe it as a random gust flutters a flower. It must seem the most natural thing in the world; she would slide it into a sentence without damaging a comma. It must be a favour; well, she would only ask them one. It must be a command; but had she not always commanded them? 'He will be a bond,' Lavinia rehearsed it – 'a visible – a sensible – a tangible memento of your kindness.' But, however she phrased it, she could imagine only one response: Mrs Kolynopulo's coarse laugh and her husband's complementary wink.

They went before breakfast. Lavinia had no time to lose. The concierges hung about together, in twos, even in threes. She must get one by himself. She must not be haughty with him, she must not let him think her afraid of him. The first one scarcely listened to her and then told her what she wanted was impossible. She withdrew to her bedroom in great agitation. The room looked as if it had slept out all night, and she could not bear to stay in it. The newspapers in the lounge were torn and dog-eared, and three days old. Envelopes, envelopes everywhere, and not a sheet of writing paper. She tried to light a cigarette, but the matches were damp, and the box, though it sprang open as if by magic and revealed a quotation from Spinoza[13], declined to strike them. One after another she tried, holding each close to the head, wearing a sore place on her finger which the flame, when it at last arrived, immediately cauterised. She gave a little cry which made everyone look at her. She hurried from the room, conscious of everything she did – the pace at which she walked, the way she held her hands, the feel of her clothes. She tried to give her movements an air of resolution; she dropped into a chair as though utterly worn out, she rose the next moment as though a thought had struck her. Then she asked another concierge, only to be told that she must wait until the gondolier came to the hotel and arrange matters with him herself. 'He will never come,' she thought. ' If he does come, someone will snap him up, and if they don't I can never make him understand.' She pictured herself conducting the negotiation, shouting to Emilio across the intervening water, while the servants and the visitors looked on. 'Oh for five minutes of Mamma,' she thought. 'How she would chivvy them! How she would send them about her business! I try to treat them as human beings; there's nothing they hate so much. They are like dogs; they know when one's afraid of them, it's the only intelligence they have.' At that moment she heard a sound at her elbow and looked up; a concierge, a tall melancholy-looking man she had not noticed before, was setting an ash-tray at her side. The simple attention confounded Lavinia; she thanked him through a mist of tears. He still hovered, gravely solicitous. Lavinia cast her line once more. Yes, he would get Emilio for her, he would telephone to the traghetto; there was no difficulty at all.

But there was a difficulty. Emilio had not returned to his station and could not be found. Throughout the day Lavinia's spirits underwent a painful alternation, rising with each effort to trace Emilio, falling when the effort proved vain. A boy was despatched to his home; even that did not bring him. He is having an orgy on the bounty of the Kolynopulos, thought Lavinia; or perhaps he has given up being a gondolier and decided to retire. No hypothesis so absurd that she could not entertain it. The explanation of his absence she never knew, but in the evening she heard he had been found and was coming to the hotel to see her.

He came. Lavinia met him in the vestibule. He was talking to the porter who, she thought, should have stood at attention or betrayed by some uneasiness his appreciation of this singular honour. But he went on arranging keys, and talking over his shoulder to Emilio, who stood just inside the street door, as though an imaginary line drawn across the matting forbade him to come further.

Through the glow of her emotion Lavinia realised, for the first time, that he was a poor man. The qualities she had endowed him with had transcended wealth and yet included it. Here, under the electric light, with the gold wallpaper behind his head and the rose-coloured rug at his feet, his poverty became a positive thing. His rings did not disguise it, and the bunch of charms and seals, supported by a gold chain and worn high up on his chest, only emphasised it. He was dressed in his everyday clothes, a sign that his term of private employment was over; they had no shape except the one he gave them. He got them because they were likely to wear well, Lavinia thought. Such a reason for choosing clothes had never occurred to her: suddenly she felt sorry for everyone who had to buy a suit because it was serviceable. But Emilio did not invite pity. He stood a little uneasily, his arms hanging loosely at his sides; he seemed anxious to subdue in himself the electric quality that leaped and glistened and vibrated. But diffidence and deference found a precarious lodging in his face: shrouded and shaded as it was, Lavinia could only glance at it and look away.

She wanted to engage him?

Why, yes, of course.

For how long?

For six days.

And when should he come?

Tonight?

No, not tonight. He shook his head as if that was asking too much.

Did she want the gondola de luxe?

Yes, she did.

'*Domani, alle dieci e mezzo?*'

'*Si, Signorina. Buona sera.*'[14]

Lavinia had to let him go at that. She would have given anything to keep him. Now that he was gone, oddly enough, she could see him much more clearly. The eye of her mind had its hesitations but it was not intimidated so readily as her physical eye. The vestibule had lost its enchantment, the hotel had reclaimed it; but she would still recall the lustre of his presence, still remember how, as he stood before her, the building at her back, civilisation's plaything, had faded from her consciousness, and the tremors and disappointments of the past days had receded with it. The hotel had grown habitable again, the servants were back in their normal stature. She passed the man who had been so helpful to her and hardly recognised him – not out of ingratitude, but because the excitement of meeting Emilio had blotted out her recollection of what went before. But the voice of disillusion whispered to her, the calendar assured her, that her time of exaltation would be short. Could she prolong it? If anyone was a judge of what was practicable, Elizabeth Templeman was she. She addressed an envelope to Miss Templeman, Hotel Excelsior et Beau Site, Rome.

My dear Elizabeth, she wrote,

I was enchanted to get your letter. What have I to set beside
your sick-room adventures? I believe that if you were at
the North Pole you could cause jealousy and heart-burning
among the very bears. My sick-room experiences (for I have
them too) are much more prosaic than yours; poor Mamma
is in bed, can't get up for several days, by doctor's orders, and
I have to look after her. But strange things happen even
in Venice, though not (as you will readily believe) to me.
My friend Simonetta Perkins (I don't think you know her –
she was recommended to Mamma, who didn't like her, so
she devolved upon me) has formed a kind of romantic
attachment with a gondolier. She is not in love with him, of
course, but she very strongly feels she doesn't want to lose sight
of him. Not to see him from time to time would be the death of
her, she says. She passionately desires to do him a good turn,
but as she has never done one before she doesn't know how to
set about it. (She is rather selfish, between ourselves.) She has
confided her plan to me, and I am passing it on to you to have
the benefit of your wordly wisdom, which is renowned in two
continents. She meditates transplanting him to America and
setting him up near her home, in some attractive occupation,
either as a baker, or clerk to a dry goods store, or something
like that. She would like it still better if she could get her
mother (who is very indulgent) to engage him as footman or
chauffeur, or gardener or even furnaceman, if he didn't
think that beneath him; then she could look after him, as it
were, herself, and see that he wasn't home-sick. She knows
a little Italian (very little considering the time she has
been here), and is very rich – she could easily transplant St
Mark's, stone by stone, she told me, if the Italian Government
would consent to let it go. I said she could do that equally well

at less expense by the exercise of faith; and she replied, quite seriously, that faith only availed to remove inanimate objects like mountains, but it couldn't bring her her gondolier – not a lock of him, not a hair.

What do you advise her to do? Of course Italians do emigrate, and it would be nicer for him to go as a private servant than settle in the Italian quarter at New York – a most horrible place. I was taken to see it once, with detectives all round me, pointing revolvers.

I do hope you are better.

Affectionately,
Lavinia Johnstone

Lavinia paused, thought for some time, then added a postscript.

Rome will soon be too hot to hold you; couldn't you flee from the wrath to come and relieve my loneliness in Venice? I am staying till Friday: it is tedious with Mother in bed and no companion but Simonetta and her obsession.

All the same, Lavinia thought, as she walked upstairs to her mother's room, I hope she won't come.

15

The midday gun boomed, but Lavinia did not hear it.

'You mean he won't come after all,' she said.

The melancholy-looking concierge shook his head.

'He came this morning at seven o'clock and said that he was very sorry, but he could not serve you. He could not hire himself to two families in turn; it would be unfair to the other gondoliers. They must have a chance.'

'I am not a family,' said Lavinia, with a touch of her old spirit.

'No, mademoiselle,' replied the concierge, looking so gravely at her that she wished she had been; her singularity sat heavily upon her. She returned to the terrace where she had been waiting the last two hours. Emilio, too, had arrived; more, he had found a fare. A woman was boarding the gondola. The gangway lurched a little as she crossed it and she turned, giving the man who followed her a smile full of apprehension and affection. She was as lovely as the day. Her companion lengthened his stride and caught her hand, and they stumbled into the gondola together, laughing at their awkwardness. The cluster of servants smiled; Emilio smiled; and Lavinia, charmed out of her wretchedness, smiled too. Into her mind came the Embarkation of St Ursula[15]; a vision of high hopes, adventure, beauty, pomp, in the morning of the world. Her smile grew wan as it lighted upon Emilio; she did not mean to recognise him, but he spread out his hands so disarmingly that the smile found its way back, flickered up again like a lamp that will burn a moment longer if you shake it.

'Who is that?' she asked at random of the servants who were still congratulating each other in a mysterious, vicarious way.

'Lord Henry de Winton,' someone said. 'They are just married.'

Lavinia went up to her mother's bedroom and stood in front of a pier-glass, studying her reflection.

'Well,' said Mrs Johnstone from the bed. 'Am I not to see your face?'

'I thought I would look at it myself,' replied Lavinia.

'Shall I tell you what you see there?' asked her mother.

'No,' Lavinia answered, and added, 'you can if you like.'

'Tears,' said Mrs Johnstone.

'I cry very easily,' Lavinia excused herself.

'As easily as a stone,' her mother rejoined.

That, alas, was only too true. Jack-the-Giant-Killer made the cheese cry by a trick, but the pressure by which the giant squeezed tears out of his stone was genuine and Lavinia could still feel the clasp of his fingers. Emilio had deserted her; he had an instinct for what was gay, what was care-free, what was splendid: a kind of ethical snobbery, she reflected, fingering the pearls that reached to her waist. She was secretive, she wore a hang-dog air, she moved stealthily in her orbit; no wonder people avoided her. She was a liar and a cheat; scratch her and you would find not blood, but a mixture of private toxins. Whereas they went blithely on their way, wearing their happiness in public, anxious that everyone they met should share it. And they had taken Emilio from her – Emilio for whose sake, or at least on whose account, she had foregone her high ironical attitude, the attitude she had spent years in acquiring, which had preserved her from so much if it had given her so little. Her detachment, that had been the marvel of her friends, how could she hope to find it now, its porcelain fragments befouled by slime? Miserably she walked up and down, her inward unrest so intense that the malign or disturbing aspects of what she saw around her contributed nothing to it. Over and over again she traced the stages of her degradation. It began with the hunt for the smelling-bottle; it was still going on: the monster inherited from the Kolynopulos had not done growing yet. 'Still,' thought Lavinia, 'if only I had engaged Emilio the first evening, I should have got what I wanted and been satisfied.' She evoked the incident a dozen times, each time saying 'yes,' where before she had said 'no,' almost cheating herself into the belief that she could alter the past. Why had he not told her last night that a trades' union scruple forbade him to enter her service? He must have thought it over, weighed her in the balance and found her wanting. How? Lavinia did not flinch from the mortification of this enquiry. She had overheard someone say she was not really beautiful. But how did her appearance affect the case? *His* appearance had affected it, but then, he was not hiring her. She did not look magnificent, not, like so many Americans, as if she was the principal visitor at Venice. The Johnstones never tried to look like that. He must have taken her meanness over the note at its face value, imagined she would always haggle over a lira. The irrelevance of this consideration, and its ironical inadequacy as the foundation of her sufferings, almost made her scream. But why, she thought, be so cynical? Emilio may not be a liar, if I am. Perhaps he did want to give the other gondoliers a chance. The benison of the thought stole through her, reinstating Emilio, reconciling her to herself. The reverie refreshed her like a sleep.

The servant who interrupted it, bringing her a card, looked as if he had been there a long while.

To introduce Lord Henry de Winton, she read, and underneath, the name of an old school-friend.

'Tell him I shall be delighted to see him,' said Lavinia.

He came soon after, his wife with him.

'Ah, Miss Johnstone,' she cried, taking Lavinia's hand, 'you can't think what a pleasure it is to find you. You must overlook the shameless haste with which we take advantage of our introduction.'

'We couldn't help it, you know,' her husband put in, smiling from one to the other. 'We had such accounts of you.'

Lavinia had been for so long seeking rather than sought after that she didn't know what to make of it.

'I hope I shall live up to my reputation,' was all she could think of to say.

If they were chilled they hardly showed it; they continued to look down upon Lavinia, kindling, melting and shining like angelic presences.

'It's hard on you, I own,' said Lady Henry. 'How much pleasanter for you to be like us with no reputation at all, not a rag!' Repudiated virtue triumphed in her eyes; but her husband said:

'You mustn't scare Miss Johnstone. Remember we were warned not to shock her.' They laughed infectiously; but a tiny dart pierced Lavinia's soul and stuck there, quivering.

'You mustn't try me too far,' she said, making an effort.

'You'll take the risk of dining with us, won't you?' Lord Henry begged. He spoke as if it were a tremendous favour, the greatest they could ask. 'And your mother too.'

'I should love to,' said Lavinia. 'Mamma, alas, is in bed.'

Instantly their faces changed, contracted into sympathy and concern.

'Oh, I am so sorry,' Lady Henry murmured. 'Perhaps you'd rather not.'

'Oh, she's not dying,' Lavinia assured them, a faint irony

60

in her tone, partly habitual, but partly, she was ashamed to realise, bitter.

They noticed it, for their eyebrows lifted even as their faces cleared.

'How tiresome for both of you,' Lady Henry said. 'Should we say eight o'clock?'

16

Why, wrote Lavinia, *when I meet the most charming people in the world should I feel like a fish out of water? The kindness of the de Wintons goes over my head. I feel like a black figure silhouetted against a sunset. The blackness is my will. I have altogether too much of it. This morning I thought it had died. My life seemed dislocated; I did the things I dislike most without minding them at all. Three hours I tramped Venice to find a propitiatory shawl for Mrs Evans. Malice governed my choice at the last; she will look a fright in it; but as I went from one shop to another, ordering its entire stock to be laid before me, and then going away without buying, I did not feel wretched and distressed, as I used to do. I didn't mind what happened. If I had been struck by lightning I shouldn't have changed colour. Things came to me mechanically, but not in any order or with any sense of choice. Volition was stilled. The de Wintons roused it. They did everything they could to draw me out, to draw me back to their level, their world where I once was, where all desires are at an equipoise, where one wants a thing moderately and forgets it directly one can't get it; where one can leave one's spiritual house, as the dove left the ark, and return to it at will. While they talked, appealing to me now and then, weaving into one fabric the separate threads of our lives, finding common interests, common acquaintances, a hundred similarities of opinion and as many dissimilarities, that should have been just as binding, drawing us together until it seemed our whole existence had passed within a few yards of each other, I felt in the midst of the exquisite witchcraft that each lasso they threw over me dissolved like a rope of sand, leaving me somewhere much lower than the*

angels, alone with my ungovernable will. It frightens me;
I cannot escape it; I cannot find my way back to that region
where diversity is real and inclination nibbles at a million
herbs and forgets the wolf, will, that watches him. Emilio is
nothing to me; he is the planetary sign, the constellation
under which my will is free to do me harm. I have devised a
remedy. Cannot I in thought identify myself with the outside
world, the world that sees with unimplicated eye Lavinia
Johnstone going about her business – notes a feather in
her hat as she stands on the terrace, sees her apparently
deep in conversation with a rough-looking man, jots down
her arrival in a newspaper, thinks she'll be gone in a week,
wonders why she doesn't change her clothes oftener, decides
after all not to trouble to speak to her? Then I should recover
my sense of proportion; I should matter as little to myself as
I do to the world.

I write like a pagan. Perhaps my disorder is more
common-place: it is the natural outcome of doing a number
of wrong things, letting myself get out of hand. Sin is the
reason of my failure with the de Wintons. The Kolynopulos'
monster, what exactly is it? It's no use going to Mamma to get
rid of it, she said so. I begin to wish that Elizabeth would
come.

Next morning the doctor was due. Lavinia stayed in to hear
his report. Each time she sought the sunshine of the terrace
she found Emilio there. His presence wounded her; his
recognitions, formal and full at first, diminished with each
encounter and then ceased. 'He has behaved badly to me,' she
thought, injured and yet glad of the injury. Though he avoided
her and grudged her his company, he could not take away from
her the fact that he, Emilio, acting responsibly with her image

in his mind, had wronged her. It was a kind of personal relation, the only one, most likely, she would have. She looked at him again. The sun shone full upon his brown neck. Surely such exposure was dangerous? Suddenly he looked up. With her hand she made a little sweeping motion behind her head. The gondolier smiled, clutched his sailor's collar with both hands and comically pressed it up to his ears, then let it fall. He pointed to the sun, shook his head slowly with an expression of contempt, smiled once more and smoothed away the creases in his collar. The Kolynopulos' monster at last came out of hiding and swam into view. Mechanically Lavinia put out her hand and took a telegram from the waiter's tray.

Earnestly advise Miss Perkins leave Venice immediately. Alas cannot join you. Writing. Elizabeth.

Lavinia crunched up the blue paper and threw it towards the canal. It was a feeble throw, the wind bore it back; so she took it to the balustrade and hurled it with all her might. It fluttered towards Emilio who made as though to catch it; but it fell short of him, and she could see it, just below the water, stealthily uncurling.

The handwriting of Lavinia's diary that night was huddled and uncouth, unlike her usual elegant script. She had been searching Venice, apparently, for a guide to conduct, or some theological work with a practical application.

Of course, she wrote, *it's only a Frenchman's view and one can't put much faith in them. I thought, if the will is corrupt, that is enough to damn you. Try to thwart the will, try to control it, try to reform it: I have tried. Faith without works is dead: that is the creed of the Roman Church and leads to indulgences. If one has faith it follows that one performs the acts of faith. Why do them? Because one can't help it. If the tree is good, so must the fruit be. And if evil? Need it be altogether evil? There's a danger in arguing from analogy; metaphors conceal truth. But suppose the tree is evil, at any one time; would it be logical to say: 'You're a bad tree; if you don't bear fruit you'll still be bad, only not so bad'? The barren fig-tree was cursed for its barrenness, not for the quality of its fruit; it may have deliberately refrained from having figs, because it knew they would be bad, and it didn't want to be known by its fruit. What I mean is, if the will is corrupt it will produce corrupt acts, and there is no virtue in refraining from any particular act, because everything you do will be wrong, wrong before you do it, wrong when you first think of it, wrong because you think it. But this man makes a distinction. To want to do wrong without doing it is concupiscence: it is in the nature of sin, but not sin. Isn't this a quibble? And it's cold comfort to be told that abstinence is concupiscence, and is in the nature of sin. I wish I could ask someone. After all, it's an academic point: I can settle it which way I like, it commits me to nothing. However I argue it I shall still believe that the act does make a difference; if I wanted to throw myself off the Woolworth building, and didn't, it would not be the same as if I wanted to and did.*

'Well, he evidently means us to get out,' said Lady Henry, looking doubtfully at the deserted campo.

Emilio was offering his arm.

Lord Henry strode ashore without availing himself of the

human hand-rail; but his wife and Lavinia accepted its aid in their transit.

'You know,' he said, 'you touch those fellows at your own risk.'

'Nonsense, Henry,' his wife protested. 'Why?'

'Oh, plague, pestilence, dirt, disease,' Lord Henry answered.

'My dear, does he look like it? He will outlive us all. Henry is secretly jealous of our gondolier,' she said, turning to Lavinia. 'Don't you think him an Adonis?'

'He is a genial-looking brigand,' said her husband.

'I was asking Miss Johnstone,' Lady Henry remarked. 'This is a matter for feminine eyes. I dote upon him.' She turned her candid eyes upon her husband with an exquisite pretence of languor.

'Well,' he gently growled, 'what about this palace? I don't see it.'

'*Gondoliere*,' called Lady Henry, '*Dove il palazzo Labia*?' She waved her hand to the grey buildings and the cloudy skies. Emilio climbed out of the boat.

'See how helpful he is,' she commented. 'He knows exactly what I mean.' Walking, Emilio always looked like an upright torpedo, as though he had been released by a mechanical contrivance and would knock down the first obstacle he met, or explode.

'We were fortunate to get him,' she continued. 'We only hold him by a legal fiction; we couldn't hire him, he has been too popular, poor fellow, all the summer, and no doubt fears the stilettos of his friends. I tried my utmost, Henry, didn't I, to shake his resolution. I spoke in every tongue, but he was deaf to them all. So we re-engage him at the end of each ride, which does just as well, and salves his troublesome conscience. Tomorrow, alas, we must go.'

They had gone down a passage and reached a door, the sullen solidity of which was impaired by the decay and neglect of centuries. Emilio pulled at the rusty bell and listened.

'Do you think,' Lavinia said suddenly, 'you could ask him to be our gondolier, Mamma's and mine, when you've finished with him? Just for two days; we leave on Friday.'

'Why, of course,' Lady Henry said.

She conducted the negotiation in her voluble broken Italian, pointed at Lavinia, pointed at herself, overrode some objection, made light of some scruple, and finally, out of the welter of questions and replies, drew forth, all raw as it were and quivering, Emilio's consent. Over his fierceness he looked a little sheepish, as though the unusual rapidity of his thoughts had outstripped his expression and left it disconnected, drolly representing an earlier mood.

The door opened and they climbed to the high formal room where Antony and Cleopatra, disembarking, stare at Antony and Cleopatra feasting.

They had tea at Florian's, under a stormy sky.

'Don't you think,' Lady Henry de Winton said, 'Miss Johnstone ought to be told some of those charming things Caroline said about her? Such a rain of dewdrops,' she added turning to Lavinia. 'I think we know you well enough.'

'Perhaps Miss Johnstone doesn't like hearing the truth about herself,' Lord Henry suggested.

'Oh, but such a truth – one could only mind not hearing it. First of all there were the general directions. Do you remember, Henry? We were not to shock her.'

'Caroline thought you were very easily shocked,' said Lord Henry, diffidently.

'She had the Puritan conscience – the only one left in

America; she might have stepped out of Mrs Field's drawing-room.'

'Really, we must talk to Miss Johnstone, not about her,' said Lord Henry, and they pulled up their chairs, turning radiant faces to Lavinia.

'And not Puritan, my dear,' Lord Henry put in. 'Fastidious, choosy.'

'I accept the amendment. Anyhow you would feel a stain like a wound. Then there were your friends.'

'What about them?' Lavinia asked.

'Oh, they were a very compact body, but they agreed in nothing except in liking you. Each one had a pedestal for you, and thought the others did not value you enough. And they were very exacting. They had a special standard for you; if you so much as wobbled, the news was written, telephoned and cabled, in fact universally discussed.'

'And universally denied,' Lord Henry said.

'Of course. But where others might steal a horse, I gathered, you mightn't look over the hedge.'

'That was only because,' Lord Henry gently took her up, 'you never wanted to look over the hedge.'

'Do you recognise yourself in the portrait, Miss Johnstone?' Lady Henry asked.

'Oh, Caroline!' Lavinia groaned.

'There's more to come,' Lady Henry pursued. 'You were inwardly simple, outwardly sophisticated. When you talked about your friends you were never malicious and yet never dull. You were a good judge of character; no one could take you in.'

'She said,' Lord Henry interpolated, with charming solicitude, 'that no one would want to.'

But his wife saw a further meaning in this well-meant

gloss and repudiated it.

'Nonsense, Henry: anyone would be delighted to take Miss Johnstone in: she must be the target of all bad characters. Caroline was praising her intelligence. There, you shall pay for interrupting me by completing the catalogue of her virtues: a formidable task.'

'Oh no,' he said, sure of his ground this time, bending upon Lavinia his bright, soft look: 'an easy one. Your poise was what your friends most admired. You took the heat out of controversies; you were a rallying point; you made other people feel at their best; you ingeminated peace.'

'How eloquent he is!' Lady Henry murmured, shaking her head.

'And yet,' he went on, 'you were a great responsibility, the only one they had. They would never let you get married; they would rush to the altar and forbid the banns. You were, you were,' he concluded lamely, 'their criterion of respectability: they couldn't afford to lose you.'

Lavinia got up. Behind her St Mark's spread out opalescent in the dusk.

'Thank you,' she said, 'and thank you for this afternoon. I must go, but before I go will you tell me what vices Caroline said I had? I know her,' she went on, looking down at them without a smile. 'She must have mentioned some.'

They looked at each other in dismay.

'Be fair,' Lavinia said, turning away. 'Think of the burden I carry, with all those recommendations round my neck.'

'We didn't mean to "give you a character",' Lord Henry's voice stressed the inverted commas.

'Couldn't you,' said Lavinia turning to them again, 'take just a little bit of it away?'

Perhaps Lady Henry was stung by her ungraciousness.

'Caroline did say,' she pronounced judicially, 'that she – that they all – wondered whether, perhaps, you weren't self-deceived: that was what helped you to keep up.'

'Not consciously deceived,' Lord Henry said, 'and they didn't want you undeceived: it was their business to see you weren't.'

They both rose. 'Goodbye,' said Lady Henry. 'It's been delightful meeting you. And may we subscribe to what Caroline said?'

Lavinia said they might.

Without much noticing where she went, she made her way over the iron bridge, past the great church of the Gesuati on to the Fondamenta delle Zattere. The causeway was thronged, chiefly it seemed by old women. Hard-faced but beautiful in the Venetian way, they moved through the mysterious twilight, themselves not mysterious at all. Even their loitering was purposeful. The long low crescent of the Giudecca enfolded the purple waters of the canal, shipping closed it on the east; but at the western end there was a gap which the level sun streamed through, a narrow strait, seeming narrower for the bulwark of a factory that defined its left-hand side. The sense of the open sea, so rare in Venice, came home to Lavinia now; she felt the gap to be a wound in the side of the city, a gash in its completeness, a false word in the incantation of its spell. She fixed her eyes on it hopefully. She was conscious of a sort of drift going by her towards the sea, not a movement of the atmosphere, but an effluence of Venice. It was as though the beauty of the town had nourished itself too long and become its own poison; and at this hour the inflammation sighed itself away. Lavinia longed to let something go from her into the drift, something that also was an inflammation of beauty and would surely join its kind. The healing gale plucked at it, caressed it, and disowned it. The sun, pierced by a gigantic post, disappeared into the sea, and at the same moment the black mass of the Bombay liner detached itself from the wharf, moved slowly across the opening and settled there. The canal was sealed from end to end.

The night was very hot. Lavinia walked to the door of the hotel that opened on the canal and leaned against the doorpost, looking out. Voices began to reach her; she recognised the tones, but the intonations seemed different.

'She's like an unlighted candle,' Lady Henry de Winton was saying. 'I can't understand it.'

'An altar-candle?' suggested her husband. 'Well, we did our best to light her.'

'No, not an altar-candle,' Lady Henry said. 'Not so living as that. A candle by a corpse.'

Lavinia tried to move away and could not.

'Didn't you find her a little un-forthcoming,' Lady Henry went on, half-injured, half-perplexed, 'and rather remote, as if she had something on her mind? She didn't seem to be enjoying herself, poor thing. We may have been enjoying ourselves too much, but I don't think it was that. Did you notice how she scarcely ever followed up what one said?'

'Perhaps she was tired,' Lord Henry said. 'She spends a lot of time looking after her mother.'

Does she? thought Lavinia.

'I could see what Caroline meant,' Lady Henry continued. 'The features were there all right, but the face wasn't. I felt so sorry for her, I longed to save her from her depression or whatever it is; I piled it on; I put words into Caroline's mouth; I perjured myself; which reminds me, my darling, that you did dot my "i"s a little too openly.'

'I tried to make what you said seem true,' Lord Henry remarked.

'Of course you did.' There was a pause in which they might have kissed each other.

'Let's forget Miss Johnstone. We've done our kind act for today.'

There was a creaking of chairs and Lavinia fled to her room.

It's no use, she wrote, after several attempts. *I cannot say what I think; I do not know what I think. I am intolerably lonely. I am in love with Emilio, I am infatuated by him: that explains me. If I can't be justified, at any rate I can be explained. Why should I hold out any longer? I am unrecognisable to myself, and to my friends. My past life has no claim on me, it doesn't stretch out a hand to me. I believed in it, I lived it as carefully as I could and it has betrayed me. If I invoked it now (I do invoke it) it wouldn't give me any help. Its experience is all fabulous; its sign-posts point to castles in Spain. Whatever happens between me and Emilio I could never find my way back to it. Respectability must lose its criterion.*

It pleased me to know that Emilio had been honest after his fashion. I can't pretend I admire him or even that I very much like him. The only creditable feeling I have is a sort of glow of the heart when he behaves less badly than I expect. These are the credentials of my passion; credential really, but the word is plural. Passion, I call it, but a shorter word describes it better. It does seem a little hard that now I have gone through so much, given up so much, I have no sense of exaltation, no impulse left. I suppose the effort of clearing the jungle of past associations has taken all my strength. I have made a desert and called it peace.

Next morning a letter accompanied Lavinia's breakfast. She opened it listlessly; she had hardly slept, and all her sensations seemed second-hand.

No, my dear Lavinia, she read, *you do not deceive me, though you do surprise me. I hope this letter will find you in America, but if it doesn't, if you have flouted my commands and are still eating your heart out in Venice, it may still serve a useful purpose. How simple you were to imagine I should be taken in by the apocryphal Miss Perkins! If you hadn't been in your weak way so catty about her, I might have thought twice about believing in her; but your letters, you know, are always crammed with things like this: 'Dear Caroline, what a saint she is, she sent me a thimble at Christmas'.*

I will now give you some rules for your guidance and I earnestly counsel you to follow them. As to your design of shipping the adored to Boston, I don't like to say what I feel about it; but this I will say: it alarmed me for you. Lavinia, you are not at all cut out for what I might call the guerrilla warfare of love. Your irregularities would be much too irregular.

Now listen to me, Simonetta Perkins, you who were once recommended to Mrs Johnstone, then rejected by her, and have now devolved upon yourself. The great thing to do is to have a programme. At ten, say, go and have a straight talk with your mother; tell her to get up, there's nothing the matter with her, and she's only wasting her time in bed. At 10.30 go to your bedroom or some inaccessible place, the roof if possible, ring the bell and tell the waiter to bring you a cocktail. Nothing is so successful in restoring one's self-respect as giving servants a great deal of trouble. At eleven, sit down and write some letters, preferably a testimonial to me saying you are following my instructions and deriving benefit. At twelve you might visit one of the larger churches. I suggest SS. Giovanni e Paolo: don't look at the church, look at the tourists, and despise them. Order your luncheon with care and see that you get what you like and like what you get. In the afternoon go to the Lido, or else buy yourself some trifle at a curiosity shop (I recommend one in the Piazzetta dei Leoncini, kept by a man with a name like a Spanish golfer, — della Torre). At five you should call on a Venetian hostess, submit to universal introduction (they will hate you if you don't and think you mal élevée), praise the present administration and listen politely to the descendants of the doges. If the flutter in your heart is still unsubdued go to Zampironi's on the way to your hotel and get some bromide: they have it on tap there. In the evening, if you haven't been asked to a party, go to Florian's and drink liqueurs – strega, I suggest. Or, if you want a shorter way to oblivion, their horrible benedictine punch. Repeat the timetable on Thursday, and on Friday, by the time your train reaches Verona, certainly when it reaches Brescia, you will have forgotten your gondolier, his name, his face, everything about him.

But whatever you do, Lavinia, don't make your plight fifty times worse by dragging morality into it. I suspect you of examining your conscience, chalking up black marks against yourself, wearing a Scarlet Letter[16] and generally working yourself into a state. Put all such notions from you. The whole thing is a question of convenience. It arises constantly, it is not at all serious. Obviously you can't marry the man; he is probably married already, and has a large family nearly as old as himself: they marry very young. If you were anyone else you might have him as a lover. I shouldn't advise it, but

74

with reasonable precautions it could be successfully carried through. But really, Lavinia, for you to have a cavalier servente *of that kind would be the greatest folly; you would reproach yourself and feel you had done wrong. And it's not a question of right and wrong, as I said: only a child of the fifties would think it was. So goodbye Lavinia, and if you can bring me a snapshot of him we will laugh over it together.*

With love,
Elizabeth Templeman

Lavinia read the letter with relief, with irritation, finally, without emotion of any kind. It was soothing to have her situation made light of; it was irritating to have it made fun of. But in proposing a solution based on reason Miss Templeman had missed the mark altogether, while her appeal to convention added another to Lavinia's store of terrors. She could face the reproaches of her friends, the intimate disapproval of her conscience; they were part of her ordinary life. But the enmity of convention was outside her experience, for she had always been its ally, marched in its van. She could not placate it because it was implacable; its function was to disapprove.

The Evanses had gone, Stephen had gone, the Kolynopulos had gone, the de Wintons had gone; Elizabeth had failed to come, and Mrs Johnstone would not rise till noon. Lavinia was alone.

Emilio did not desert her; he came in all his finery, he was delighted to see her. Stepping into the gondola Lavinia felt almost satisfied. It was a prize she had fought for against odds during a fortnight, and at last it was hers. '*Comandi, Signorina?*' Emilio said, slowly moving his oar backwards and forwards. 'Am I his Anthea[17]?' thought Lavinia. 'Can I command him anything?' But she only suggested they should go to San Salvatore. '*Chiesa molto bella*,' she hazarded. '*Si, si*,' returned Emilio, '*e molto antica*.'[18] That was the sort of conversation she liked, so easy, like fitting together two halves of a proverb. She felt deliciously weary. Suddenly she heard a shout. Emilio answered it, more loquaciously than was his wont. She looked up: it was only a passing gondolier, saying good-morning. Another shout. This time a whole sentence followed, in those clipped syllables which Lavinia could never catch. Emilio ceased rowing and answered at length, speaking in short bursts and with great conviction. A minute later a similar, even longer, interchange took place. The whole army of gondoliers seemed to take an interest in Emilio, to know his business and to be congratulating him on some success. Suddenly it seemed to Lavinia that from every pavement, traghetto, doorstep, and window a fire of enquiries was being directed upon her gondolier; and the enquirers all looked at her.

'It's my imagination,' she thought; but in the afternoon the same thing happened again; it was like a nightmare. Convention, even Venetian convention, was showing its teeth, growling through the walls of its glass house. Lavinia was seized with a contempt for all these people, mopping and mowing and poking their noses into other people's business. 'What are they,' she thought, 'this population of Lascars and Dagoes?' For a moment she felt Emilio to belong to them, a rift opened between her and him: she saw him as it were through the wrong end of a telescope, minute, insignificant, menial, not worth a thought. In his place appeared all the generations of the Johnstones, sincere, simple, grave from the performance of municipal and even higher functions, servants of their own time, benefactors of the time to come.

They were the people upon whom America had depended; America owed everything to them. From the sixteen-thirties when they arrived until the beginnings of vulgarisation in the eighteen-eighties, for two hundred and fifty years they had persisted, an aristocracy unconscious of its own aristocratic principle, homely, solid, and affluent. If they remembered their descent – and Lavinia could recollect every generation of hers – they remembered it historically, not personally: the matter of genealogy was common knowledge: it was a bond to hold them together, not a standard for others to fall short of. It was domestic, this society to which they belonged, it was respectable, it was as democratic as an aristocracy could well be. And still, though threatened on all sides by an undifferentiated plutocracy, it kept its character, it preserved its primness, its scrupulosity, its air of something home-made and old-fashioned, without gloss or glitter. The lives of rich people now-a-days tended to follow the line of least resistance. They could go where they wanted, see what they wanted, do what they wanted; but the range of their desires was miserably contracted; with them personality was a mere drop in the bucket of prosperity. If they possessed a Gainsborough, they only possessed a name. 'But if we have a Gainsborough,' Lavinia mused, 'we are not thereby debarred cherishing the lines of the family tea-pot; and it would hurt me more to lose my grandmother's brooch than my pearl necklace.' 'That is it,' she continued, elated, feeling herself necessary to civilisation: 'we have not lost touch with small things although we have an intimacy that does not need to wear its heart upon its sleeve or barter its secrets in the open market.' Higher and higher mounted the tide of her self-complacency. For days the mood had been a stranger to her; now she encouraged it, indulged it, exulted in it, thinking, in her buoyancy, it would never leave her.

'We didn't take things lightly,' she boasted, 'we made life hard for ourselves. We thought that prosperity followed a good conscience, not, as they think now, that a good conscience follows prosperity. We did not find an excuse for wickedness in high places.' Unaccountably the rhythm of her thought faltered; it had felt itself free of the heavens, but it was singed, and drooped earthward with damaged wing. 'If Hester Prynne[19] had lived in Venice,' she thought, 'she needn't have stood in the pillory.' For a moment she wished that Hawthorne's heroine could have found a country more congenial to her temperament. 'It was my ancestors who punished her,' she thought. 'They had to: they had to stick at something. One must mind something, or else the savour goes out of life, and it stinks.' She glanced uneasily round the room. It had taken back its friendship and had an air of lying in wait for her to disgrace herself. 'Take that,' she muttered, slamming the wardrobe door. But it swung back at her, as though something inside wanted to have a look. 'All right,' she threatened, 'gim-crack stuff in a paste-board palazzo. At home, if I shut a door, it shuts.' But the brave words didn't convince her, and when she tried to visualise her home, she couldn't. The breakdown in her imaginative faculty alarmed her. Suppose that, for the remainder of her life, when she wanted to evoke an image, it wouldn't come? Tentatively, not committing herself to too great an effort, she trained her mind's eye upon the portrait of her great-aunt, Sophia. There was a blur, then a blank: and in turn, as she called upon them, each of the portraits evaded her summons. 'It is unkind of you,' she murmured, almost in tears, 'after I have given you all such a good character.' Then suddenly, as her mind relaxed, the images she had striven for flooded uncontrollably into it, bending their disapproving stare upon her, proclaiming their hostility.

Who was she to commend them? Small thanks would they have given her for her praise: they could only relish a compliment if it came from a virtuous person. They wouldn't want her even to agree with them: they would distrust their very thoughts if she said she shared them. In whom, then, could she confide and to whom could she go for help? Not to the dead and gone Johnstones, for by no act of renunciation could she ingratiate herself with them. She could plume herself with their prestige if she liked; they could not stop her making a snob of herself. But any closer identification, any claim on their long-preserved integrity, any assumption that she, for what she should now give up, was entitled to take her place beside them – this, their grave displeased faces, still circling about her, positively forbade. She might trade on their name, but their goodwill, the vitality of their tradition, could never be hers. They disowned her.

'Well, let them go,' thought Lavinia. 'In the face of life, what use is a recipe from the past? I have fed myself too long upon illusions to want to add another to them.' She was aware of the grapes going sour; in her mouth was a bitter, salty taste; in her eyes the vision of her fate, limitless, agoraphobic, its last barricade thrown down; in her ears, perhaps, defunctive music, the leave-taking of the gods she loved.

The glory of the Johnstones seemed to crumble; root, branch, and stem they were stricken and the virtue passed out of them. She walked up and down the room, conscious of an amazing exhilaration. The rivers of her being, long forced uphill, turned back upon themselves, joined and flowed away unhindered in one dark current. At last she had reached a state of mind that did not need working for, that could be maintained without effort, that absorbed her and left nothing over. The sense of being at odds with herself disappeared;

the general awareness of friction and unease that had subtly cramped her movements as well as her thought slid from her; her very skin lay more lightly on her.

'I am lost!' Lavinia cried. It was a moment of ecstasy, but it passed and she burst into tears.

'Well, I don't want you to go, but you must be back by eleven. Remember we've got to get up early.' Lavinia heard her mother's voice, the firm voice of the recovered Mrs Johnstone, but it sounded a long way off. She closed her bedroom door and locked it.

' "*Amo*" is all right,' she muttered, fluttering the leaves of a dictionary, 'though it has a smack of the Latin Grammar, but should I say "io" too? "Io" is emphatic, it might be taken to mean that I love him but other people don't; "Io ti amo": "I love you to the exclusion of" – and that would offend him and be silly besides: everyone must love him. "*Ti amo, ti amo*", I must remember that.' Lavinia breathed quickly and lay down for a moment on her bed. She rose, restless, and looked at the place where she had lain. There was a small depression, scarcely noticeable, and the pillow had filled out again. 'I make very little mark,' she said to herself, and the thought, absurdly enough, filled her with self-pity. She went to the looking-glass and stared at her face as though she would never see it again. 'I ought to have had a photograph taken,' she thought inconsequently. 'I could have done: I had time.' Still standing in front of the mirror she opened her purse; it was empty. Quickly she went to a box, fidgeted with the key and walked slowly back, a bunch of notes in her hand. One by one she stuffed them in her purse. 'Another?' she muttered and looking up, met her questioning eyes in the glass. She shuddered and walked unsteadily into a corner of the room behind the wardrobe, as though it were not enough to keep out of her own sight. To the intruder she unconsciously feared, she would have presented the appearance of a naughty child, taking its punishment. 'One more?' she muttered, in her new, stifled voice. 'How can I tell?'

'*Comandi, Signorina?*' Emilio asked. Lavinia started. '*Alla musica,*' she said, '*e poi, al Canal grande della Giudecca.*'[20]

They drifted slowly towards the swaying lanterns, and drew up alongside another gondola. The Toreador's song blared across the water; a man was singing it also, at the second barge, the serenata of St Mark, only a few hundred feet away. The unfortunate coincidence gave Lavinia a feeling of insanity. The song became a kind of canon; each singer paused to hear where the other had got; the little orchestra hesitated, scraped, decided to go on. Lavinia could not endure it. '*Alla Giudecca,*' she said.

'*Va bene, Signorina.*'

The canal opened out, very black and very still. They passed under the shadow of a trawler.

'*Ferma qui,*'[21] said Lavinia suddenly.

The gondola stopped.

'Emilio,' Lavinia said, '*Ti amo.*'

'*Comandi, Signorina?*' murmured the gondolier, absently.

'I shall have to say it again,' thought Lavinia.

This time he heard, and understood.

At what time would she like to be home?

At eleven.

'*Impossibile.*'

At half-past eleven?

'*Si, Signorina.*'

Rapidly the gondola pressed its way alongside the Fondamenta della Zattere. With each stroke it shivered and thrilled. They turned into a little canal, turned again into a smaller one, almost a ditch. The V-shaped ripple of the gondola clucked and sucked at the walls of crumbling tenements. Ever and again the prow slapped the water with a clopping sound that, each time she heard it, stung Lavinia's nerves like a box on the ear. She was afraid to look back, but in her mind's eye she could see, repeated again and again, the arrested rocking movement of the gondolier. The alternation of stroke and recovery became dreadful to her, suggesting no more what was useful or romantic, but proclaiming a crude physical sufficiency, at once relentless and unwilling. It came to her overwhelmingly that physical energy was dangerous and cruel, just in so far as it was free; there flashed across her mind the straining bodies in Tiepolo and Tintoretto[22], one wielding an axe, another tugging at a rope, a third heaving the Cross aloft, a fourth turning his sword upon the Innocents. And Emilio with his hands clasping the oar was such another; a minister at her martyrdom.

She strove to rid her mind of symbols. 'The oar is just a lever,' she thought. ' "We have the long arm of the lever over here. The long arm of the lever – the long arm of the lever".' The silly words stuck in her head like a refrain. Still, with unabated pace, the gondola pushed on. Which side would it stop? 'It'll be this one,' she thought, catching sight of some steps dully outlined against the darkness. 'No, not that, this.' A dozen times apprehension was succeeded by relief. 'I'm having a run of luck,' she told herself, her mind confusedly adverting to the gaming tables: 'perhaps I shall get off after all.' But let the red turn up as often as it liked, one day the black would win. The odds were against her. But there were no odds; the die was cast. The solace of independent thought, that stuffs out with its bright colours whatever crevices of the mind the tide of misery has forgotten to fill, was taken from her. A wall of darkness, thought-proof and rigid like a fire-curtain, rattled down upon her consciousness. She was cut off from herself; a kind of fizzing, a ghastly mental effervescence, started in her head.

It suddenly seemed to Lavinia that she was going down a tunnel that grew smaller and smaller; something was after her. She ran, she crawled; she flung herself on her face, she wriggled…

'*Gondoliere*!' she cried, '*Torniamo al hotel.*'

'*Subito Signorina?*'

'*Subito, subito.*'[23]

The next morning Lavinia was sitting by her mother's side in the Orient express. They had been travelling some hours. The train pulled up at a station.

'Brescia?' she thought. 'Why do I remember Brescia? But Elizabeth was wrong. I shall never forget him.'

NOTES

1. 'How can I help?' (Venetian dialect).

2. Writer and art critic John Ruskin (1819–1900); Venetian painter Vittore Carpaccio (c.1460–c.1525).

3. Samuel Richardson's eight-volume epistolary novel, *Clarissa* (1748–9).

4. Giovanni Bellini (c.1430–1516) was the leading Venetian painter of his time.

5. Sing-Sing Prison near the Hudson River was completed in 1828; it has strong connotations with the electric chair.

6. The line 'Cast the bantling on the rocks' is from 'Self-Reliance' by Ralph Waldo Emerson (1803–82).

7. The line 'I cannot praise a fugitive and cloistered virtue' is from Milton's *Areopagitica: A Speech of Mr John Milton for the Liberty of Unlicensed Printing to the Parliament of England* (1644).

8. Poet and critic F.W.H. Myers (1843–1901).

9. Venetian streets.

10. Jezebel, a Baal worshipper, used her position as Queen of Israel to persecute the Hebrew prophets. She was eventually punished by being thrown from a window, whereupon, in fulfilment of a prophecy, her body was eaten by dogs (I Kings 16–21 & II Kings 9).

11. Presumably a reference to E.M. Forster's *A Room with a View* (1908), which opens in Italy.

12. The line 'Mummy was once merchandise – Mizraim cured wounds – Pharaoh was sold for balsams' is a quotation from *Hydriotaphia* (1658) by philosopher and physician Sir Thomas Browne (1605–82).

13. Philosopher and theologian Benedictus de Spinoza (1632–77) was a leading Rationalist thinker.

14. 'Tomorrow, at half-past ten?'

'Yes, *Signorina*. Goodbye.'

15. The painting *Seaport with the Embarkation of St Ursula* (1639) by Claude Lorrain (1600–82).

16. A reference to Nathaniel Hawthorne's *The Scarlet Letter* (1850), in which the heroine is put in the pillory and forced to wear a red letter A for committing adultery.

17. Anthea was an epithet of the Greek goddess, Hera, the queen of the gods.

18. Lavinia's stilted Italian means 'Church very nice.' Emilio responds 'and very old'.

19. The heroine of *The Scarlet Letter* (see note 16 above).

20. 'To the music… and then to the Great Canal in the *Giudecca* [Jewish Quarter].'

21. 'Stop here'.

22. Giovanni Battista Tiepolo (1696–1770) was the last of the great Venetian painters; Tintoretto (1518–94) is best known for his sacred murals.

23. 'Go back to the hotel.'
'Immediately, *Signorina*?'
'Immediately, immediately'.

Leslie Poles Hartley was born in Wittlesey, Cambridgeshire, in 1895, the son of a solicitor. He was educated at Harrow, before going on to Balliol College, Oxford. During the First World War, he enlisted in the Army although he never went on active service.

Hartley began his literary career as a short-story writer and reviewer; he was a contributor for such publications as the *Spectator* and the *Observer* for in excess of thirty years. His first book, *Night Fears*, a collection of short stories, was published in 1924, followed, in 1925, by *Simonetta Perkins*, a novella set in Venice, one of Hartley's most favoured places. Following the publication of *Simonetta Perkins*, Hartley was acclaimed by the *Saturday Review* as 'one of the most hopeful young talents that the last few years have revealed to the reading public'. His first full-length novel, *The Shrimp and the Anemone*, however, did not appear until 1944. This was the first part of a trilogy, the remaining parts, *The Sixth Heaven* and *Eustace and Hilda*, appearing in 1946 and 1947 respectively. *Eustace and Hilda* was awarded the James Tait Black Memorial Prize and it is by this title that the trilogy is generally known. Hartley's most famous work, *The Go-Between* (1953), received the Heinemann Foundation Prize of the Royal Society of Literature, and was later made into an extremely successful film. His other novels include *A Perfect Woman* (1955), *The Hireling* (1957) and *My Sister's Keeper* (1970), and he also published a collection of lectures and critical essays, *The Novelist's Responsibility* (1967).

Hartley was awarded a CBE in the New Year's Honours List in 1956. He died in 1972, shortly before his seventy-seventh birthday.

SELECTED TITLES FROM HESPERUS PRESS

Author	Title	Foreword writer
Louisa May Alcott	*Behind a Mask*	Doris Lessing
Pedro Antonio de Alarcon	*The Three-Cornered Hat*	
Pietro Aretino	*The School of Whoredom*	Paul Bailey
Jane Austen	*Love and Friendship*	Fay Weldon
Honoré de Balzac	*Colonel Chabert*	A.N. Wilson
Charles Baudelaire	*On Wine and Hashish*	Margaret Drabble
Aphra Behn	*The Lover's Watch*	
Giovanni Boccaccio	*Life of Dante*	A.N. Wilson
Charlotte Brontë	*The Green Dwarf*	Libby Purves
Mikhail Bulgakov	*The Fatal Eggs*	Doris Lessing
Giacomo Casanova	*The Duel*	Tim Parks
Miguel de Cervantes	*The Dialogue of the Dogs*	Ben Okri
Anton Chekhov	*The Story of a Nobody*	Louis de Bernières
Anton Chekhov	*Three Years*	William Fiennes
Wilkie Collins	*Who Killed Zebedee?*	Martin Jarvis
Arthur Conan Doyle	*The Tragedy of the Korosko*	Tony Robinson
William Congreve	*Incognita*	Peter Ackroyd
Joseph Conrad	*Heart of Darkness*	A.N. Wilson
Joseph Conrad	*The Return*	Colm Tóibín
Gabriele D'Annunzio	*The Book of the Virgins*	Tim Parks
Dante Alighieri	*New Life*	Louis de Bernières
Daniel Defoe	*The King of Pirates*	Peter Ackroyd
Marquis de Sade	*Incest*	Janet Street-Porter
Charles Dickens	*The Haunted House*	Peter Ackroyd
Charles Dickens	*A House to Let*	
Fyodor Dostoevsky	*The Double*	Jeremy Dyson
Fyodor Dostoevsky	*Poor People*	Charlotte Hobson
Joseph von Eichendorff	*Life of a Good-for-nothing*	
George Eliot	*Amos Barton*	Matthew Sweet

Henry Fielding	*Jonathan Wild the Great*	Peter Ackroyd
F. Scott Fitzgerald	*The Rich Boy*	John Updike
Gustave Flaubert	*Memoirs of a Madman*	Germaine Greer
E.M. Forster	*Arctic Summer*	Anita Desai
Ugo Foscolo	*Last Letters of Jacopo Ortis*	Valerio Massimo Manfredi
Giuseppe Garibaldi	*My Life*	Tim Parks
Elizabeth Gaskell	*Lois the Witch*	Jenny Uglow
Théophile Gautier	*The Jinx*	Gilbert Adair
André Gide	*Theseus*	
Nikolai Gogol	*The Squabble*	Patrick McCabe
Thomas Hardy	*Fellow-Townsmen*	Emma Tennant
Nathaniel Hawthorne	*Rappaccini's Daughter*	Simon Schama
E.T.A. Hoffmann	*Mademoiselle de Scudéri*	Gilbert Adair
Victor Hugo	*The Last Day of a Condemned Man*	Libby Purves
Joris-Karl Huysmans	*With the Flow*	Simon Callow
Henry James	*In the Cage*	Libby Purves
Franz Kafka	*Metamorphosis*	Martin Jarvis
John Keats	*Fugitive Poems*	Andrew Motion
Heinrich von Kleist	*The Marquise of O–*	Andrew Miller
D.H. Lawrence	*Daughters of the Vicar*	Anita Desai
D.H. Lawrence	*The Fox*	Doris Lessing
Leonardo da Vinci	*Prophecies*	Eraldo Affinati
Giacomo Leopardi	*Thoughts*	Edoardo Albinati
Nikolai Leskov	*Lady Macbeth of Mtsensk*	Gilbert Adair
Niccolò Machiavelli	*Life of Castruccio Castracani*	Richard Overy
Katherine Mansfield	*In a German Pension*	Linda Grant
Guy de Maupassant	*Butterball*	Germaine Greer
Lorenzino de Medici	*An Apology for a Murder*	Tim Parks
Herman Melville	*The Enchanted Isles*	Margaret Drabble
Prosper Mérimée	*Carmen*	Philip Pullman